Tales of Hope and Redemption

by

Russell Hatler

and

Hope Morgan

Published by Lulu.com

Copyright@2022 by Russell K. Hatler

ALL RIGHTS RESERVED

No part of this publication may be reproduced, stored in a retrieval system or transmitted in any form or by any means--whether virtual, electronic, mechanical, photocopying, recording, or otherwise--without the written permission of the copyright owner.

ISBN 978-1-79470-322-3

Contents

Hope Earns Her Stripes 1
Partly Cloudy with a Chance of Chelsea 12
Hope Rolls the Dice 21
You Make Me Feel So Young 26
Hope Lets the Dogs Out 51
Burner Phone 58
May Ruth Pays the Price 77
Silent Witness 83
Hope Loses Faith 93
Tell Laura I Love Her 100
Hope Abides 117
The Coromandel Armoire 136
Hope Gets Hinky 153
The Flesh is Willing 160
Hope Plays with Fire 173
Trust 180
Hope Calls It a Day 203
Acknowledgments 211

Hope Earns Her Stripes

Hope Kennedy (no relation to John F. although, had Hope been born forty years earlier and a thousand miles north there's a good possibility they would've had a relationship. According to an article published in the New England Journal of Medicine, female pheromones can be transmitted over a sizeable distance. Let's say as impressionable adolescents, Jack and Hope were strolling mindlessly through the mall and their paths crossed. Even at a young age Hope had a luscious figure. And Jack was a male. And Jack was rich!); anyhow the eponymous Hope Kennedy graduated from Pender High School in Burgaw, North Carolina, when she was sixteen. Hope had great grades and a wholesome smile. Problem was Hope Kennedy grew up poor.

Hope lived with her mother and grandfather in a doublewide situated within walking distance of Pender High School. Hope loved the fifteen-minute walk to school. A school bus stop was located down the road. Hope used the bus in inclement weather, but she preferred the solitude of her walk.

When Hope was three, a stranger came to the back door of her parents' little farmhouse, asking for a handout. Hope's mother took pity on the stranger and invited him in for lunch. When they'd finished eating the stranger pulled out a gun, shot her father and raped her mother, escaping down the road in their five-year-old Pontiac station wagon. Hope doesn't remember the details, only that they moved into the doublewide with her grandfather shortly after the incident and that her mother was sad for a long time.

Hope didn't have a lot of close friends growing up. She frankly preferred the company of adults. She was best friends with the high school career development coordinator, Miss Frances Higgins, who introduced Hope to the Pell Grant program during her junior year.

"What's a Pell Grant?" asked Hope. "And why would I be interested?"

"I presume you plan on going to college after you graduate," replied Miss Higgins, looking up from her computer monitor. "I just Googled it. UNCW participates in the program. First you file an FAFSA form. Then, based on your EFC, you may be eligible for aid."

"What's a Google?" asked Hope, glancing around the edge of the desk at Miss Higgins' computer monitor. "And what's the rest of all this alphabet soup bullshit?"

"Google is the search engine used by the Yahoo web browser," said Miss Higgins. "If you're going to swear at least close the door."

Hope got up and shut the office door. Then she scooted her fold-up guest chair around to Miss Higgins' side of the desk so she could see better.

"What's Yahoo?" asked Hope. "And what's a web browser?"

"Don't go off-topic," said Miss Higgins. "Mr. Aronson is teaching a computer basics class next semester. I strongly encourage you to take it. Take typing too in case the Pell Grant application doesn't work out. That way at least you can qualify for a job as a secretary."

"Okay, cool," said Hope. "Then what's an FAFSA?"

"That stands for Free Application for Federal Student Aid," replied Miss Higgins patiently. "And EFC stands for Expected Family Contribution. There's a formula they use to figure out how much your family can contribute towards your college education. That determines your eligibility for FAFSA which in turn is used to calculate your annual Pell Grant award."

"Piece of cake," grinned Hope. "My family doesn't expect to contribute anything to my continuing education. In fact, once I graduate Pender High my mother plans to boot my pretty little ass out the door."

"You do plan to go on to UNCW, though, don't you?" asked Miss Higgins, concern etched on her face. "You have the highest GPA in this year's junior class. Among girls, that is. A couple of the jocks have higher GPAs, but we all know why that is."

Miss Higgins was a dedicated feminist before it was fashionable to be that sort of person. The female students thought she was a bit dyke-like in the bargain. Hope didn't give a shit. She liked Miss Higgins.

"Yahoo the FAFSA form and let's fill it out," said Hope. "How much time will it take?"

"You can't fill out the form until you enroll in college," explained Miss Higgins. "You can't enroll in college until you graduate high school. You won't graduate high school for two more years."

"Fuck that shit," said Hope. "Why can't I graduate this year instead of next year?"

"Right now, it's the beginning of the first semester of your junior year," said Miss Higgins. "I think had we had this discussion two years ago you might've been able to finish in three years. Now it's highly unlikely. There are too many required courses and too little time."

"Yahoo me up a list of requirements and let's talk turkey," said Hope enthusiastically. "I love a challenge."

"You do understand it'll seriously impact your social life," advised Miss Higgins.

"My social life these days is fuck all anyhow," said Hope. "Let's get this show on the road."

As it turned out Hope was right. It was possible to graduate in three years although, as she put it later in life, it felt like she'd been "dipped in shit and hung out to dry." She didn't get much support from her mother or grandfather. They agreed between themselves that she was nuts. Killing herself just so she could go to a fancy University with all those hoity toity rich folks just to get bounced out when they decided to show her who was the boss. And then she'd end up a secretary just like God intended in the first place.

After graduation (she ranked fifth in her graduating class even though she was by far the youngest student) Hope enrolled at UNCW with the help of Miss Higgins, who believed counselors had an obligation to help their students, regardless of whether or not they were still in school. As soon as she was accepted, she and Miss Higgins filled out the requisite forms and applied for the FAFSA along with the Pell Grant. Hope's EFC was sufficiently modest that she ended up qualifying for the whole enchilada, which she figured would get her through college without batting an eye.

She was wrong. Hope fell in with the wrong crowd. They weren't evil people bent on overthrowing the system. They were idealists who fervently believed in the humane treatment of animals, especially animals of the canine species. Shortly after she arrived at UNCW Hope joined ARF! (the Animal Rescue Fellowship) and soon discovered that charity work sometimes demands a certain amount of discretionary funds. One of her fellow ARF! Members, a junior from Charlotte named Addie Franklin who was majoring in Political Science, told Hope over late night beers in Addie's off-campus, one-bedroom apartment, that she supplemented her meager funds from home with a little nocturnal dalliance engaged in for cash on the barrelhead with a cadre of gentleman movers and shakers from the upper echelons of Wilmington society. On her back, so to speak.

"Oh, come on, Addie," said Hope. "That's easy for you. You're gorgeous with tits out to here. I'm skinny as a stick!"

"How old are you, Hope?" teased Addie. "Undernourished as you may appear, I'll bet you still managed to get some boy to bust your cherry in Burgaw. Tell your big sister the truth."

"I'll be seventeen in June," Hope admitted. "And you're right, I did. But it wasn't as straight forward as you think. For one thing Pender County boys don't have a great deal of imagination. For another it's not easy to find any privacy in a doublewide. But in the end, I managed to entice one bedraggled nerd out behind the proverbial barn and get him naked. Once you've got their pants off the rest comes easy."

"Speaking of tits," said Addie. "Take off your shirt. I want to show you something."

Hope had had just enough beer that Addie's idea didn't seem bizarre. She gingerly pulled her T-shirt off over her head.

"Take off your sports bra too," encouraged Addie, unbuttoning her blouse. "It's just us girls."

Hope obliged as Addie unfastened her own double D cup brassiere. Addie's awesome breasts came tumbling out. Hope let out a gasp. Addie reached over and tweaked Hope's left nipple. The little rascal snapped to attention.

"Now that's mighty admirable sensitivity," smiled Addie. "I've always said responsive nipples are worth their weight in gold. A man once said anything you can't get in your mouth at one time is a waste. I concur. May I?"

Hope nodded, Addie slid a nipple between her lips and proceeded to perform a miracle. Hope had never been with anyone who knew the proper way to stimulate a nipple. It was delightful. Addie stopped way too soon. She lay back on the bed, pulled up her skirt, pulled off her panties and motioned to Hope.

"Now you," she urged, cupping one enormous breast in her right hand. "Panties off."

Hope complied. She was surprised to find that Addie's nipples weren't nearly as responsive as her own. Nonetheless they were forbidden fruit and therefore a guilty joy to fondle. And delicious to taste. Hope felt Addie's hand grasp hers. Addie eased Hope's hand down to her secret place. Oh my! Addie was already incredibly wet. That's when Hope discovered there are many ways to skin a cat. Or, to put it more precisely, there are many pursuable paths and byways that can make a pussy purr.

After the deed was done and they lay naked in each other's arms, Addie sighed deeply.

"Either you're a quick learner or you're a full-blown, natural, down and dirty sex goddess," she grinned. "So, here's the deal. Several of my clients have expressed an interest in a *Ménage à Trois*. You're perfect. Pliable, responsive and smart. Oh, and being jailbait is not necessarily a liability. Some guys get off on underage girls. We double the price and split the proceeds fifty-fifty. Deal?"

"Do we have to do this again?" asked Hope coyly. "In front of an audience? Maybe we need to practice some more before we make that decision."

When the evening was over, they both felt they'd made enormous progress. Addie started getting in touch with her clients the very next day. Needless to say, the *Ménage à Trois* girls were a clandestine hit throughout the entire Cape Fear Region. And Hope Kennedy was no longer strapped for cash.

Which was not necessarily a blessing because the extra income led to Hope sampling other aspects of urban life which had been heretofore inaccessible. Like Grass, Ecstasy, and Coke, coupled with the occasional rave. Underground Wilmington, at the dawn of the twenty-first century, was beginning to embrace the rave, even as enthusiasm throughout the rest of the nation was beginning to wane. Indeed, a wag once remarked that the North Carolina rave is easily distinguished by its vinegar flavored MDMA.

Ecstasy was amazing. It made Hope tingle with a sexual thrill, the magnitude of which she'd never been able to achieve with beans and franks alone. Or with another girl, for that matter. Since her personal and commercial relationship with Addie, Hope had become sexually flexible to a fault.

Ecstasy also made Hope feel like the world was the best place to be in ever, even though she knew our judicial and political systems were seriously fucked up. When she was eighteen, in the MDMA-enriched aftermath of one particular rave, Hope got pregnant by a boy named Howard Goodall from Myrtle Beach. Howard's parents took custody of the baby girl shortly after she was born. They named her Faith Ann after a favorite aunt.

Hope was powerless to challenge their legal claims. Hope was single and a student with no visible means of support. Howard's parents were comfortably well off. They were also well acquainted with a well-respected firm of litigation attorneys. Howard's mom had always wanted a daughter. Now she had one. They did grudgingly consent to allow Hope to visit the little girl whenever the mood struck her. Knowing the toll drugs take on a user they presumed Hope would soon forget about the baby. They were wrong. Hope thought about her baby every waking moment of every day.

As far as Hope's own mother and grandfather were concerned, the Goodall parents' adoption of Faith Ann was a blessing in disguise. They figured maybe it would bring the girl to her senses. Get married and settle down. Come back to Burgaw and help out at the annual blueberry festival. Like any good daughter should.

    Hope had other plans that most definitely did not include blueberries. She didn't want to be the girl a boy brought home to his parents. She wanted to be the girl his parents warned him about!

Partly Cloudy with a Chance of Chelsea

Chelsea Ann was the second smartest student in her senior class at Permian High School in Odessa fucking Texas. Oh, not UTPB smart. Chelsea harbored no illusions about going on to a higher education after graduation. Chelsea prided herself on being street smart. She got good grades, to be sure. She had a B+ average. But university life wasn't for Chelsea. Chelsea had other fish to fry.

Chelsea's mom, Paula May Harrison, dropped out of Odessa High in the middle of her junior year, by which time she was already four months pregnant with Chelsea. Chelsea's father, Randolph Applewhite, was a feed and grain salesman who lived over in Abilene. At least that's what he told Paula May when they were dating. Well, dating wasn't exactly the right word. Paula May and Randy met at church one Sunday where Paula May taught Sunday School. Randy had a meeting with the local John Deere dealer Monday morning at 8:00 and he didn't want to get up at 5:00 and drive all the way into Odessa so he bit the bullet, drove up Sunday morning in time to make the 11:00 church service and stayed overnight at the local Motel Six.

Paula May was what you might call mature for her age. Her bustline had begun to develop by the time she was ten, for God's sake, and by the time she was a sophomore she had tits out to here! Paula May's mom used to bind Paula's breasts with a dishtowel so nobody would notice but everyone knew what was going on. Paula May got her period when she was thirteen. She started teaching Sunday School shortly after her fifteenth birthday. One thing you had to give the girl, Paula May sure did know her Bible.

Paula May and Randy hit it off right away. They shared an avid interest in films, especially the latest crop of spy thrillers out of Hollywood. When it came to musical tastes, Paula May loved Pearl Jam whereas Randy had a thing for Nine Inch Nails and so one thing led to another and Paula May ended up spending the night in Randy's hotel room after telling her parents she was sleeping over with a friend from school, Sally Carter. And that one thing that led to another led inexorably to Chelsea.

Paula May started her house cleaning service when Chelsea was one. It's hard to find gainful employment when you have a one-year-old daughter. It's even harder when you don't have a high school diploma or even a GED. Paula May applied at a dozen fast food joints around town and all she got for her trouble was free fries, a bunch of empty promises and the offer of twenty bucks for a blow job if she'd do it bare.

Paula May's mom reluctantly took care of her granddaughter while Paula May was at work. Paula May's dad did her taxes and helped out with the bills when he could which wasn't all that often. Nonetheless Paula May's house cleaning service was a modest success. After a couple of years, she was obliged to bring on three fulltime Hispanic ladies whose green cards wouldn't necessarily stand up to close scrutiny and a bookkeeping service that helped send out the bills and bank the checks.

When Chelsea was seven her grandmother passed, something to do with a rare blood disease, and Paula May was forced to put Chelsea in day care after school during the week and bring Chelsea to work with her on weekends. By the time Chelsea was nine she'd gotten pretty good at emptying wastepaper baskets and scrubbing bathtubs.

Federal law prohibits teenagers aged fourteen and fifteen from working during school hours so Chelsea couldn't very well get officially involved in the business but Paula May had a special relationship with Francis Olson, the principal at Permian High, so he turned a blind eye when Chelsea regularly showed up for class at 11:00. Between 8:00 and 10:30 Chelsea pitched in with the house cleaning chores. Paula May paid her daughter under the table. The bookkeeping service didn't know about the cash customers and Paula May wasn't about to rat them out.

Chelsea had been a member in good standing of the Permian High cheerleader's squad since her sophomore year. Practice sessions were held after school was out. Chelsea inherited her mother's aforementioned voluptuous bustline, which went a long way toward keeping Chelsea's membership active and vibrant. During the fall quarter of her junior year Chelsea met and began dating one of the offensive linemen for the Permian Panthers, Cletus "Clete" Sanderson. Clete wasn't the sharpest knife in the drawer, but he was good hearted, and he cared for Chelsea a lot. By the time summer rolled around they were going steady.

Here's the problem. Chelsea was so good at her job Paula May had given her complete responsibility for five of her regular customers. She'd also given Chelsea a used Electric Bicycle for her sixteenth birthday so she could easily get to and from her clients' houses. Chelsea loved the bike. The obligatory bike helmet not so much. It mashed down her hair and made her look stupid.

Chelsea found she could do one house in three hours. Less if there wasn't a lot of dust. Dust was the killer. Fortunately, the houses Paula gave her to do were occupied by middle-aged, married couples with neither pets nor children. Kids and dogs were the primary culprits when it came to dust. Furthermore, the houses themselves were less than fifteen minutes away by bike from Chelsea's place. If Chelsea left her place at 7:30 she could do one house and still be at school by 11:00. Chelsea did the Graham house on Monday, the Ferguson house on Tuesday, the Wilson house on Wednesday, the Johnson house on Thursday and the Smith house on Friday.

Sandy Graham taught third grade at Reagan Elementary School. She had to be at work by 8:00. Sandy's husband, Alex, worked swing shift at a meat packing plant. He didn't normally get up before 10:00. Sandy had given Chelsea a key so she wouldn't have to awaken Alex. One Monday morning Chelsea biked to the Graham house, unlocked the front door, and walked into the kitchen. She heard a strange noise down the hall. It sounded like someone was in a great deal of stress. She tiptoed down the hall and peeked into the guest bedroom. Alex Graham was perched precariously on the edge of a high back, brown leather armchair, a frayed orange towel spread across his naked thighs, masturbating furiously into a pair of lady's lace panties. Now Chelsea wasn't born yesterday. She'd taken a course in Human Sexuality. Furthermore, she fancied herself to be an enlightened, customer-centric businesswoman. So instead of gasping and crying out she strolled over to the sofa and asked quietly, "Could you use a hand?"

To which Alex wheezed," Oh God Yes! Please."

Chelsea carefully removed her clothing, everything except for her panties, knelt on the plush carpet and proceeded to finish Alex off. Then she washed her hands, put her clothes back on and returned to the kitchen. Fifteen minutes later Alex walked sheepishly into the kitchen and slipped a hundred-dollar bill into the pocket of Chelsea's apron. Mondays thereafter were particularly profitable for Chelsea.

Margaret Ferguson was a cashier at the downtown branch of the Community National Bank. She had to be at work by 8:30 so the bank could open at 9:00. Margaret's husband, Felix, was a used car salesman. His work hours were erratic. Felix was a closet fetishist. He liked to dress up in women's lingerie and leather boots. Chelsea surprised him one Tuesday morning, smiled pleasantly and helped him fasten a pesky brassiere snap he was having trouble with. Then she complimented Felix on his taste in women's delicate undergarments. She even went so far as to unbutton her blouse and show Felix how abundantly she filled out her own sturdy bra. Felix was uncommonly grateful. Tuesdays thereafter were particularly profitable for Chelsea.

And so on through the week. It turned out Arnie Wilson, a prominent attorney, liked to have his temperature taken. Chelsea invested $500 in a nurse's uniform and a rather large rectal thermometer for which she was not only reimbursed, but handsomely rewarded as well. The other two husbands had more pedestrian tastes. The only rules were "no touching, panties on and absolute discretion." Given Chelsea's tender age and the marital and social status of each of her special clients there was ample incentive to abide by the rules. But in light of her newly acquired wealth, which she kept in a secret compartment of her Gucci purse, Chelsea had taken to carrying a pearl-handled derringer just in case.

By the end of their senior year together, Clete's innate biological urges were becoming increasingly demanding. Chelsea had never had a problem manually satisfying Clete's animal lust, but she was saving herself for marriage. Clete, on the other hand, had also taken the class on Human Sexuality. He knew what a burden involuntary celibacy could become to the male of the species if it was allowed to flourish. He'd seen pictures of deformed genitalia. He'd heard tales of men driven mad by their carnal cravings. He was determined not to let that happen to him.

And so one night, after a particularly ugly loss on the gridiron, Clete drove his Ford F350 to the ridge behind Permian High where a thick grove of trees masked the amorous activities of ardent lovers and parked in a secluded spot. While Chelsea was in the process of "giving Clete a hand" in the rear seat of Clete's Ford F350, Clete ripped off her panties, pulled her out of the truck, splayed her unceremoniously out on the pine-needle-strewn earth and proceeded to fuck the shit out of her. When he was finished, he rolled off Chelsea's ravished body, heaved a sigh of relief and began to snore.

Chelsea stood up, dusted the pine needles from her posterior and opened the passenger side door. She removed the pearl-handled derringer from her Gucci purse, squatted awkwardly on the ground and put a bullet through Clete's thick skull. Then one more for good measure. She rifled through the pockets of Clete's jeans, found the ignition keys to the truck, put her clothes back on, bid farewell to Odessa fucking Texas, and drove off into the night.

She'd always wanted to visit Las Vegas. Now seemed like as good a time as any. Despite the lateness of the hour Chelsea felt surprisingly refreshed. She could phone her mom from Albuquerque around dawn, catch forty winks at a rest stop, grab a snack, get back on the road and ditch the pickup on the outskirts of Vegas. Uber into town and find a room at a local motel that rented by the week. All things considered, Chelsea was a happy girl.

Hope Rolls the Dice

What with raves, pharmaceuticals, three-ways (they tried a four-way once, but the third girl just wasn't into it and she kept knocking the guy's glasses off), and class work, Hope's college days went whooshing past. Burgaw was a long way off and Hope didn't have a car. She did get Addie to drive her there one weekend, but it was a disaster. Her grandfather ogled Addie the entire Saturday afternoon and her mother treated Addie like a freak, referring to her as "Hope's little girlfriend," which perhaps she was but that sort of behavior was frowned on up in Burgaw!

Given her new, lucrative sideline, Hope had honestly expected to be able to put away a substantial nest egg but by her junior year the daily average balance in the UNCW student special combined checking and savings account she'd opened at Wells Fargo with the earnings from her first romp ($175) was $175. She did have several eye-catching outfits and a new bike, but no matter how diligently she tried to save money it just kept slipping away.

ARF! was certainly one of the problems. By her junior year Hope was deeply involved in the day-to-day operation and financing of the fellowship; scheduling rallies, paying the bills, and drafting posters and notices to pin on grocery store message boards regarding the sorry plight of our furry friends. Somebody had to pay for the materials and legwork, not to mention the fees for printing and distribution. They also had big plans for a summer convention for ardent poodle lovers but that fell through when the city council decided against officially supporting their cause. It seems the City of Wilmington actually made money from the animal shelters ARF! was protesting against. Not much to be sure but the fact that 50% of the "rescued" animals were euthanized spoke volumes about the phony code word "shelter!"

Another niggling fiscal peccadillo surfaced while Hope and Addie were basking in the afterglow of a threesome with a gentleman who'd just had his bells rung. Twice! Charlie Easterman was the dude's name.

"I don't suppose either of you two girls gamble," Charlie said. "Probably not. I don't think Bambi (Hope's *nom de plume*) is old enough and Jennifer (Addie's Backpage handle) is far too practical. But there's a big Casino Ship party this weekend down in Little River. I scored three complimentary tickets to the festivities. I'm taking the wife. Maybe you know somebody who'd like to use the spare ticket?"

As luck would have it Hope had a fake ID, complete with sober faced picture, that attested to the fact that she was twenty-three. When they first started to work the *Ménage à Trois* ploy, Addie had introduced Hope to a guy who worked magic on legitimate documents. Hope invested the requisite $500 and had aged four years overnight. Ain't technology grand?

"I'd love to, sir," said Hope meekly. Hope was playing the worshipful sub this particular Wednesday evening. She and Addie traded off. "I'm not as young as I appear although I appreciate the compliment."

Charlie got out of bed and grabbed his pants.

"Here's the ticket," he said, handing it to Hope. "There's a shuttle bus that runs between Wilmington and Little River on weekends. You probably don't want to drive. The traffic's gonna be horrendous." He handed Addie the agreed-upon $350 for their time together spent indulging in mutually beneficial activities. Then he handed Hope another hundred-dollar bill.

"Play a roll of quarters for me," he grinned lasciviously. "Next time I see you two let me know how it worked out."

"Same time next week, Charlie?" asked Addie playfully. "You know how we love to see you."

"I do indeed," smiled Charlie, stepping into his pants. "And I know how much Junior here loves to see you girls too! Even though he only has one eye."

They all got a good chuckle out of that.

Hope was thrilled. She'd never been on a gambling ship before. On Saturday morning she caught the bus downtown to Thalian Hall, walked across the street to the library and waited for the shuttle bus to Little River, South Carolina. She was half an hour early. She didn't care. She had her backpack book bag filled with textbooks. If she ran out of gambling money, she wanted to be able at least to study topside, out there in the salty air. The gambling money from her savings account was in her purse along with the hundred-dollar bill she'd gotten from Charlie. Who knows? She might double or even triple her stash. It could happen!

The bus trip was uneventful. Hope sat way in the back. Up front were seven old ladies who'd obviously done this sort of thing before. They chitchatted back and forth with the driver. Hope studied while they rode. Basic Bookkeeping Principles. Her head was so full of Debits and

Credits and Assets and Liabilities she could scream. Nonetheless it was a welcome departure from staring at a banker's package. Charlie Easterman was a nice guy compared to some of their other clients, but he did have an ego as big as, well, you know. Bigger than, actually.

The bus pulled into the parking lot in Little River. The eight passengers and the driver disembarked. The passengers went into the half-filled waiting room. Hope poured herself a complimentary glass of pink lemonade. They had another forty-five minutes before the ship sailed. On the book rack next to the cash register was a dog-eared paperback titled "All You Need To Know To Win At Craps." Hope grabbed the book. Beat the shit out of Basic Bookkeeping. By the time the ship sailed, Hope was an expert.

Hope did not become a gazillionaire on her first casino cruise, but she did become hooked on craps. She became a regular on the shuttle bus down to Little River. She never won big but now and again she broke even. And it wasn't as if she didn't have the money to lose. She was careful never to let her bank balance get below $175. That way she figured she was always ahead of the game.

You Make Me Feel So Young

Misty Manson perched precariously on a wooden stool beside the brown, Naugahyde massage table that had been pushed up against the wall of her basement office in the Springville, North Carolina, town hall. It was 8:25 on a Monday evening. The nether-folds of her tight, white cotton pants described the image of a delightful camel toe. It may have been somewhat uncomfortable, but the suggestive silhouette did bring in the big bucks. Misty was naked from the waist up, hardly the couturial protocol one might associate with a professional physical therapist. But she was young and lovely.

Gerald Kramer, age 73 and counting, sprawled face up on the massage table, his Tommy Bahama shirt unbuttoned to the waist, and his knee-length, black satin gym shorts snugged up over his bony knees. Gerald was neither young nor lovely, but he did have a few points going for him. He was comfortably well off, retired, widowed and generous to a fault. Gerry wasn't millionaire rich, but he was no longer obliged to pinch pennies. Misty was taking Gerry's blood pressure.

"A man walks into a bar and sits down beside a beautiful blond," said Gerry, staring up at the ceiling. "He pulls a frog out of his pocket and sets it on the bar.

'This is a very special frog,' the man whispers to the blond.

'Looks like a regular frog to me,' replies the blond. 'What's so special about your frog?'

'This frog eats pussy,' says the guy with a big grin. 'I taught him how myself!'

'I don't believe it,' scoffs the blond.

'Hike up your skirt,' says the guy. 'And slip off your panties.'

The blond does so. The frog just sits there. The guy shakes his head sadly.

'Okay,' he says. 'I'm gonna show you one more time...'"

Gerry let out a gleeful snort. Misty blushed prettily, pinched Gerald hard on his left nipple and said, "Why Mr. Kramer, that's really naughty!" To which Gerry grinned, rolled over on his right side, and slipped another twenty into Misty's overflowing tip jar.

Springville, population 31,416, is a sleepy bedroom community situated roughly forty miles northeast of Raleigh. The diverse citizenry of Springville is comprised of farmers, tradespeople, technicians, and retired executives who spent the bulk of their careers in Research Triangle Park, the high-tech capital of the Southeast. Five years back, when the town's coffers were in great shape, the city fathers decided to position Springville as the most desirable retirement destination in Eastern North Carolina. To that end they hired a Public Relations firm from Fuquay-Varina to devise a scheme that would help them realize their dream. The PR guys took a survey and determined that what Springville needed most was a Senior Wellness Center.

At that time the town hall had a sizeable basement that had been used primarily for document storage. Since most of the documents had been digitized and stored in a cloud database, the basement was mostly vacant. What an ideal location for a Senior Wellness Center.

Now all they needed was to hire somebody who was uniquely qualified to run the place, preferably a somebody who wouldn't cost the town an arm and a leg. They sent a recruitment team of one, namely Emory Bridgeford, down to UNC Chapel Hill in search of the ideal candidate. Emory was a retired high school Social Studies teacher whose nephew was mayor of Springville. Emory had never married but he did know a thing or two about Wellness Centers. He was a lifelong member of the YMCA.

Emory searched far and wide for a qualified candidate. He decided early on the candidate needn't have a PhD in Physical Therapy, although UNC had the best program in the country. A Master's would suffice. That alone knocked $15,000 off the starting salary. He was also looking for a female. Knock off another $10,000. Now we're talking. In the end his search boiled down to five candidates, three of whom were already gainfully employed by Planet Fitness. He finally settled on Misty Manson, a fully qualified physical therapist who also sported a mighty fine figure. Even though Emory had never married he was nevertheless a card-carrying, male, heterosexual. Mighty fine indeed.

Misty had her undergraduate degree in Biological Science and her Master's in Physical Therapy from UNC Chapel Hill. She'd hoped to complete her PhD but her Sugar Daddy died and the money ran out. Her Sugar Daddy's name was Lemuel Forrester. Lem Forrester developed the generalized algorithm for data mining. Every time you click on a link on your phone or laptop LFDMA, llc, gets a tenth of a penny. It adds up!

Lem once told Misty that when he was a younger man, he'd placed first and third in a circle jerk contest. Those were the good days. Lem's wife of thirty-five years died of ovarian cancer. Those were the bad days. Misty helped Lem get over the bad days. And she helped him re-experience the good days. After a fashion.

Misty accepted Emory's offer on the spot. The decision wasn't difficult. Since her premature ejaculation from the student population at UNC, Misty had toiled at a number of temporary jobs, none of which utilized her physical therapist skills. Most recently she was a day-shift lap dancer at the Triangle Cabaret. The tips were good, but the employee benefits program sucked.

It turned out Misty was a pretty good organizer. Once she was settled in an apartment in Springville, she went straight to work. She cleaned out the town hall basement, ordered ten exercise bikes, four Stairmasters and three treadmills. Then she sat down with a local architect. Together they laid out individual offices with floor-to-ceiling walls for Misty and three assistants. They also penciled in male and female dressing rooms, male and female shower areas, and a reception desk.

As an incentive to recruit qualified assistants, Misty ordered top of the line laptops for each of the four offices. The town had an IT department. Misty cajoled the department head into lashing the laptops together into a Local Area Network so the assistants could play computer games against each other during lulls in the action. When the town council saw the bill for the whole shebang, they had second thoughts, but they were already committed. The Springville Senior Wellness Center was the centerfold of their advertising campaign. And Misty Manson was Playmate of the Decade.

For the first couple of years Misty was content to bank her paycheck and run the show. Operating hours were 9:00 to 5:00 five days a week. Misty and her staff showed up at 8:00 every morning to get things started. But then one day on her way to work she blew out the engine in her 2012 Honda Civic, and when she checked her bank balance, she realized something had to change. That's when she came up with the idea for the Happy Rascals.

Every resident of Springville over the age of 55 was automatically a member of the Springville Senior Wellness Center. The expenses of the Senior Center came out of the town budget. Members were charged $25 per visit, which included an unlimited supply of bottles of water, a locker for their street clothes, personalized fitness programs and hot showers after workouts. T-shirts, caps and gym shorts were sold at the reception desk. All things considered the Springville Senior Wellness Center pretty much paid for itself.

Misty's staff consisted of three associates, a receptionist, and a part time bookkeeper who also handled the Human Resource stuff. Misty reported directly to the Town Manager, Harry Whitehead, who gave her free rein over the operation. Harry had other fish to fry. He had his hopes pinned on a much more lucrative position down in the Triangle but so far Harry hadn't had much luck in getting somebody to sponsor him. This was primarily because Harry had a closet drinking problem which exacerbated his issue with anger management, which was itself related to his attitude towards women, but it wasn't all Harry's fault. He'd had an overbearing mom and his dad left town for greener pastures when Harry was five.

Misty's three assistants, two female and one male, were under the age of 35. They were all trained as physical therapists although only the male, Tommy, had an advanced degree. Of the females, Linda had a BA in Biological Sciences from ECU and Mary Beth had an undergraduate degree in History and Political Science from Duke. All three were personable and hardworking but when the clock struck 5:00 they had better things to do than hang around old people.

The town council's Public Relations campaign seemed to be working. After two years over twenty percent of the town's permanent residents were eligible for membership in the Senior Wellness Center, a hundred fifty of whom were weekly participants in the program. Another two hundred showed up from time to time to run on the treadmills and dish the local dirt. At the outset of the operation geriatric males outnumbered geriatric females two to one although more and more women seemed to be showing up as the elderly population grew.

Misty not only managed her assistants, she worked alongside them. She had a few favorites among her growing roster of male clientele, one of whom was Gerald Kramer. Gerry had been there from the beginning of the Wellness Center program. He was a retired Senior Programmer from IBM. He'd started out his illustrious career as a third shift operator back in the day when computers were bulky mainframes and worked his way up to become a top-notch systems programmer.

Gerry's wife, Marge, died in a boating accident on Jordan Lake the year after Gerry retired. When Gerry came across an article on the Springville PR campaign in the local rag, he drove north to see what the fuss was all about. He loved the relaxed pace of Springville. He loved the idea of a Senior Wellness Center. And he was secretly enthralled with Misty even though he was a good forty years older than she was. He sold up and moved to Springville where he was destined to become the leader of the band.

"You look a little out of sorts this morning, sweetheart," said Gerry, sitting on a metal folding chair across the desk from Misty.

"My damn car broke down on the way to work this morning, Mr. Kramer," Misty said, shaking her head. "Excuse my French. I just got a call from the repair shop. They said it'll cost $1,600 to fix the engine. I don't have a spare $1,600 laying around. And even if I did, after they fix it, it'll still be a damn 2012 Honda Civic."

"I wish I could help you out of your dilemma," said Gerry. "I could loan you the $1,600 but that wouldn't fix the real problem. Short of marrying a dot com millionaire, I can't think of a lot of options when it comes to improving your financial prospects long term. Not in Springville, anyhow. I'm sure the town council would go bat shit crazy if you asked them for a raise. Just thinking out loud, but how much do you think it would take to get you out of the hole?"

Misty thought for a moment.

"$600 a week tax free would do the trick," she said thoughtfully. "That's what I used to make in tips down in the Triangle. I'm afraid I have a bit of a checkered past, Mr. Kramer. I don't mind sharing my secret with you, but I'd appreciate it if you didn't mention it to any of my friends or colleagues."

Misty went on the explain her dubious job description when she worked at the Triangle Cabaret before being hired to run the Senior Wellness Center. Gerry listened to her tawdry tale. Gerry was a good listener. He was also more than a tad bit aroused by her plight. And her potential. Nor did Gerry get easily aroused these days.

"So, if we get six guys, counting me, to kick in $100 a week to improve your financial situation that would make you whole?" asked Gerry. "I think that's doable. What kind of incentive might we offer in exchange for their pecuniary expression of good will?"

"I think we could promise to provide some one-on-one, hands-on stimulation to improve their outlook on life," said Misty. "All in the name of wellness, of course."

"I don't think we should offer to provide this special service during normal business hours, do you?" asked Gerry. "Loose lips sink ships and all that."

"Say six guys, forty-five minutes each max, fifteen minutes between sessions to clean up after," said Misty, doing the math. "I'm pretty sure I could provide special needs services between 7:00 and 9:30 three nights a week. If a guy achieves his personal goal a few minutes early, so much the better."

"I'll recruit the other five core candidates," said Gerry. "I can be your guinea pig until we fine tune the process. The seven of us, you included, will form the nucleus of the operation. The inner circle if you will. Once the word gets out, I'm sure there will be lots of other guys who are eager to join in on the fun. You get with the town council to schedule the special needs time slots. I think we need a name for our group of special needs clients. Let's call them The Happy Rascals."

"What do you hope to get out of this, Mr. Kramer?" asked Misty suspiciously. "And Happy Rascals works for me."

"The honest satisfaction that comes from helping a fellow human being out of a jam," said Gerry with a grin. "Plus of course the joy of periodically achieving my own personal goal."

"If I'm gonna pitch this to management, don't you think we need a more sophisticated-sounding title than Happy

Rascals?" asked Misty. "Something that sounds vaguely scientific."

"Good point," replied Gerry. "How about Holistic Rejuvenation? I think that covers all the bases."

"I'll run it up the flagpole and see if Harry salutes," said Misty with a grin. "Wish me luck."

Misty went upstairs and walked down the hall to Harry Whitehead's office. Harry was busy updating a bunch of Excel spreadsheets on his laptop. He glanced up and motioned Misty to enter. She came in and sat down. Misty explained what she and Gerry had in mind, omitting the salient details. She used the phrase Holistic Rejuvenation several times, as if it were a term of common usage within the scientific community.

"Isn't that really what we're all about here at the Senior Wellness Center?" she asked. "About putting the spring back in a man's step. In a woman's step too, come to that."

Harry was in one of his rare, good moods. He toggled over to the balance sheet for the Senior Wellness Center and noticed that, in addition to goodwill, they'd generated a cool $160,347 in revenue during the past two years, not counting T-shirts and caps. The town hall was shuttered after 6:00 pm, for all practical purposes, so space was available. Of course, they'd have to engineer secure access to the basement area with card keys and pass codes but that wasn't impossible. He gave Misty provisional approval to proceed with a nominal budget of $10,000. He suggested a start date three weeks hence. Misty agreed. Misty went back down to her office where Gerry was just hanging up the phone.

"Mr. Kramer," she smiled. "We have Harry Whitehead's permission to go ahead with The Holistic Rejuvenation project. I'm excited."

"Great!" said Gerry, tapping his finger on an open notebook. "I have our other five guys signed up already. Fred Rogers is a retired construction worker from Durham. You'll like Fred. He comes across as kind of crude when you first meet him, but Fred's okay. Next there's Lou Masters. Lou spent his early life teaching high school English. Lou and Fred are widowers. The third guy's named Jimmie Silver. Jimmie sold insurance for a living. Never married but he did have a live-in girlfriend for seven years, so he obviously appreciates the feminine touch."

Gerry paused to take a breath.

"Fourth guy's Desmond Willis," he continued. "Des is diabetic, divorced and has a pet Golden Retriever. I have no idea what Des did for a living, but he's loaded. The fifth guy is Reginald Roundtree. Reggie's also a widower. He wasn't my first choice, but I think he'll come around. He drives a luxurious White Cloud Electric Vehicle and generally lives way beyond his means. Spent his career in middle management at IBM. I worked as a techie under Reggie for two years. Reggie takes full credit for everything his minions accomplish. I didn't like it. Maybe life has changed him. At least he can afford the price of admission. How about we meet for a drink after work and firm up the plan? No strings attached. There's a nice place on Mill Street. Say 5:30?"

"Maybe you forgot, Mr. Kramer," pouted the forlorn Misty. "I'm stranded. No wheels. That's what this Holistic Rejuvenation exercise is all about."

"I have an idea," said Gerry, consulting his watch. "I know this car rental place in Rocky Mount. Nothing fancy but the rates are reasonable. How about we drive up for lunch and rent you a compact after? I presume a week will give the shop plenty of time to get your car back on the road."

"That's very generous of you, Mr. Kramer," sighed Misty. "But you're forgetting something else. I don't have the $1,600 to get the car fixed."

"I'll give you an advance to cover the cost of my Holistic Rejuvenation sessions," grinned Gerry. "$100 a pop, three times a week, we should be able to work off the $1,600 in a little over a month if we count tips. Make sure you include budget for a tip jar, by the way. Men do the strangest things when they're basking in the afterglow of achieving a personal goal."

"Deal," said Misty with a grin. "But don't go getting any funny ideas. I hardly know you."

"Heavy on the hardly, Misty," smiled Gerry. "Grab your bonnet and let's go get fed!"

Lunch was at a Mexican place across from the park in Rocky Mount. It was delightful. After lunch Gerry wiped his mouth on a napkin, reached across the table and took Misty's hand.

"We need to be clear about something before we kick this whole thing off," he said. "We've got the inner circle nailed down, but down the road we need to keep the target population of Happy Rascals to a bare minimum. What we're proposing isn't precisely illegal but some of the townsfolk in Springville are a trifle conservative. The fewer guys we invite to participate the better off we are. I know my gender. Once word gets out, I have a feeling we'll be inundated by applicants. What do we do then?"

"Too many potential clients is a good problem to have," said Misty. "But I do see your point. I know how many guys I can comfortably handle in a week. No pun intended. If we were down in Raleigh, there's no shortage of co-eds who'd leap at the chance to lend a hand. But up here I'm not sure where we go to recruit talent. Most of the ladies in town are either retired and arthritic, they're stay at home housewives or too young for us to talk to."

"Somebody once said even stay at home housewives have fantasies," said Gerry. "I suspect those fantasies generally include engaging in a titillating spate of illicit sex with a stranger, but I don't think they necessarily include engaging in a titillating spate of illicit sex with an elderly stranger. On the other hand, I'm sure every bored housewife in town could use a few extra bucks in her cookie jar."

"If we have to hire a regimen of raw recruits to supplement the sensual bliss delivered by my tender touch, we'll need a hierarchy of skill sets," said Misty. "Let's call our trainees HR Acolytes. Once they become proficient, they get promoted to HR Practitioners. Eventually the crème de la crème may rise to the level of HR Meritrician."

"Brilliant," said Gerry. "And we could set session rates and tip recommendations based on the skill level of the HR professional providing the service."

"Didn't I hear a story about some guy in town who got a mail order bride from Thailand?" asked Misty. "Phuket, I believe they said."

"It's pronounced Poo-Ket," said Gerry gleefully. "Wash your mouth out."

"Jonathan Wilkerson," said Misty, pointedly ignoring Gerry. "His mail order bride's name was Nana. After three years of marital bliss, Jonathan Wilkerson ran off to Atlanta with his secretary. I think an interview with Nana Wilkerson is in the cards. Nana Wilkerson could be our first HR Acolyte."

"Probably be a good idea to sound her out before we get too deeply involved," said Gerry. "Would you like for me to do the interview?"

"It's best if I handle that delicate task," sniffed Misty. "I'm not entirely convinced of your ability to draw an unbiased conclusion. Like asking a fox to impartially assess the egg-laying talent in a henhouse."

"I am shocked, Ms. Manson, shocked!" said Gerry, but he was secretly relieved. He wasn't sure his body rub interviewing techniques were up to date. "Let's go get your rental car."

Nana Wilkerson was a treat to interview. She was petite, polite, accommodating and delightfully submissive. Furthermore, she confessed that she was intimately familiar with the ticking of a man's testosterone-fueled inner

42

clockwork and admitted in hushed tones that she knew the best way to guiltlessly alleviate his stress.

Nana worked days cleaning houses in and around Springville. She had two coworkers of Hispanic descent who might be amenable to contributing to the Holistic Rejuvenation project. Yes, she was willing to train them if Misty thought that would help. In fact, Nana was willing to demonstrate her skills on Misty right now if she was so disposed. They were equally effective on the female of the species, although the delivery technique varied of necessity. Misty said she'd take a rain check, and could Nana start work next week? Nana said she'd love to.

Six months later the Holistic Rejuvenation project was up and cooking. Misty had hired seven Acolytes and promoted three of them to Practitioners. She and Gerry set the going price per half hour session at $25 for an Acolyte, $50 for a Practitioner and $75 for a Meritrician. Misty was the sole Meritrician so far, but Nana wasn't far behind. They also suggested a tip of $100 per session, more if the level of individual satisfaction warranted. Happiness at the Senior Wellness Center was on the rise and tip jars were overflowing.

At 6:15 on a Monday evening Misty was in her office preparing for the nocturnal onslaught of Happy Rascals. The night's dance card was filled, with menfolk waiting in the wings in case somebody called in and cancelled. Came a knock at Misty's door. She opened it. Standing outside, hat in hand, was a member of the Oxford County constabulary. In the back of her mind Misty had always known this day would come but she wasn't quite yet ready to be arrested. Things were going so well.

"Come in, Officer," said Misty. "How can I help?"

"My name is Race Carson," said the cop, ambling into the room. "I've heard rumors about certain activities hereabouts and I was curious to know what's going on."

"Nothing illegal, I assure you," said Misty.

"That's not what I meant," stammered the officer. "I'm not here in an official capacity. But my sister-in-law, Melanie, might be able to help you folks out."

It turned out Melanie was recently widowed. Her husband Fred, Race's brother, had got killed in a car crash up in Rocky Mount five months back. The family didn't have much cash and Melanie had four kids to support. Race heard there might be work for an enterprising young woman and he wondered if Misty might want Melanie's contact information. Well Misty sure would like to talk to Melanie whenever it was convenient. As luck would have it, Melanie was sitting outside in Race's cop car right now.

Race went back out and brought Melanie in. Now Melanie wasn't much to look at, but Misty could see she was a damsel in distress and Misty was a soft touch, so she ushered Race out into the hall, closed the office door, sat Melanie down and did the whole fifty cent interview. A good thing she did, too, because Melanie possessed a skill set that was unique. Melanie specialized in stimulating the frenulum.

"I'm not sure what a frenulum is," said Misty. "Can you enlighten me?"

"Sure can, sweetheart," said Melanie. "You know that flap of skin under the head of a man's penis? That there's a frenulum. It's real sensitive to a woman's touch if she knows how to touch it. Perks up a man's pee-pee something fierce. I used to bring old Fred to attention on a nightly basis. Old Fred, he never complained."

"I could see how that might solidify a marital relationship," said Misty pensively. "But I'm not sure how it applies within the context of Holistic Rejuvenation."

"It seems to me you're ignoring half your potential customers," said Melanie. "Frenulums aren't restricted to menfolk. Womenfolk have frenulums too. Tucked up deep inside their female parts. I've never tried my stimulation technique on a female frenulum, but I can't imagine it wouldn't do the trick. All I'm asking is a chance to try."

Which led to the formation of the Happy Rachels, a distaff group that convened Tuesdays and Thursdays in the basement of the Springville town hall. The best part was it turned out Melanie's frenulum-stimulating skills weren't entirely a matter of hereditary. They could be taught. Soon the entire HR staff were fully trained in male and female frenulum stimulation. And the happiness level of Springville Seniors soared.

Wednesday afternoon three months later. Gerry Kramer knocked on Misty Manson's office door.

"Come in," Misty sobbed.

"What is it, Misty?" asked Gerry, coming in and closing the door.

She handed Gerry an envelope. Inside the envelope was an 8 ½ X 11 grainy black and white photograph. The photograph showed Misty perched on the wooden stool, reaching toward Gerry who was sprawled on the massage table. You could just make out the curve of Misty's naked breast. The caption on the photo read "Gerald Kramer, a Happy Rascal whose Nipple Misty Pinched." Attached to the photo was a post-it note that read "$10,000 keeps the secret, Refusal breaks the bond. The Oxford County

Register Gazette would love to spread the news. Delivery details to follow shortly."

"What the fuck?" muttered Gerry, sitting in the guest chair. "I thought what we did in your office was private. Where did this picture come from?"

"I have no idea," said Misty. "But if the newspaper gets hold of this, we're sunk. I don't know what to do."

"Let's think this thing through," said Gerry studying the photo. "The angle rules out an overhead spy cam. In fact, the only possible lens must have been situated on your desk. Hang on a second."

He got up and went around to Misty's side of the desk. Her laptop was open.

"Did you know your laptop has two camera lenses? One looking back at you and the other looking in the opposite direction. Looks to me like somebody took a picture using the outward facing lens. No wait. Not a picture. This looks like a still frame from a video. Shit! Scoot over. I need to look at your hard drive storage."

Misty went around her desk and sat in the guest chair while Gerry rifled through the contents of Misty's hard drive.

"Son of a bitch!" Gerry exclaimed. "He's been recording all your Holistic Rejuvenation sessions. Wait here."

Gerry went into the office next door. When he came back, he was shaking his head.

"Next door too," he said, sitting back down on Misty's desk chair. "Looks like somebody's been taping everything that goes on behind closed doors. Fuck! Let me think for a minute."

Gerry scratched his head. Then he began typing away furiously on Misty's keyboard. After a while he stopped and smiled.

"Gotcha!"

"What is it? Or rather should I say who is it?"

"I don't have a name, but I do have an IP Address," said Gerry. "I can see the device that was used to select the camera lens and activate the recording app. And I'm pretty sure I can guess who owns it. We need to call a meeting of the inner circle. Now."

Thirty minutes later the inner circle was assembled in Misty's office. It was cramped as hell. Gerry and Misty were behind Misty's desk. Fred Rogers sat in the guest chair. Lou Masters stood next to Fred. Jimmie Silver and Desmond Willis sat on the massage table. Reggie Roundtree stood beside the closed door.

"One of you twisted shits is trying to blackmail Ms. Manson," said Gerry, pulling out his iPhone. "I don't know which one it is, but I'll tell you this straight out. Ms. Manson is under the protective custody of The Dancer, and nobody fucks with The Dancer."

Gerry scrolled down to his contacts list and selected a number. He clicked on the number. Reggie's phone rang.

"Gotcha!" exclaimed Gerry.

Reggie bolted from the room, exited the basement through the after-hours door, jumped in his White Cloud, burned rubber, and headed off down the road. Gerry shook his head sadly.

"I never did trust that son of a bitch," he said.

"What are we going to do?" wailed Misty. "He's got the photo, he's headed to the Oxford County Register Gazette, and he's sure as Hell gonna blow our cover. We're all fucked!"

Fred, Lou, Jimmie and Des just looked bewildered.

"I don't fucking think so," said Gerry. "Watch this."

He tapped an icon on his iPhone. The screen was filled with the scene of a dusty country road. Misty realized she was looking at the live feed from the forward-facing camera on Reggie's White Cloud. Gerry tapped on a Joystick Controller icon at the top of the iPhone screen. Four Arrow Buttons and an ENTER Button were superimposed on the screen. Gerry tapped the ENTER Button. Then he tapped the UP-Arrow Button. The White Cloud accelerated. Gerry tapped the RIGHT-Arrow Button. The White Cloud veered sharply to the right and barreled straight into a large oak tree. The screen went blank.

"Nobody fucks with The Dancer," Gerry said, pocketing his iPhone.

"I think I love you," said Misty. "Dancer."

Hope Lets the Dogs Out

It wasn't until Hope's senior year that the shit hit the fan. As far as her courses were going, she was doing great. Even though she hadn't amassed a fortune in her bank account she was still above water. She thoroughly enjoyed her professional and personal relationship with Addie, who had completed her bachelor's degree and was now pursuing her master's in Poly Sci. The problem related to ARF!

New Hanover County Animal Control was a division of the Sheriff's office. They were overworked and understaffed. Most of the people who worked there were kind and caring folks but there's only so much you can do when you're short of resources. Citizens didn't adopt frequently enough. Feral pets weren't neutered. Nor were their offspring. Old dogs and cats weren't adoptable. The list goes on and on. The last thing these people needed was helpful advice from a bunch of well-meaning college kids.

On the other hand, the pet-centric members of ARF!, the majority of whom were dog lovers, were sick and tired of being ignored. To be fair, it's a fact that stray cats comprise a larger percentage of animal shelter inmates than dogs and a significantly larger percentage of the cats are euthanized. But dogs are easier to love. At least according to Hope. Nor was Hope the kind of gal who was content to sit around and let nature take its course. She wanted action. Now!

It was the middle of spring semester, mid-April. The Wilmington Azalea Festival was scheduled for the coming weekend. Tourists were already pouring into town. Hotel rooms had been booked for months. Stray pets were picked up nightly, discreetly of course. If a handful of those incarcerated strays had legitimate owners, no biggie. The owners could damned well come down to Division Drive and retrieve their recalcitrant animals. No sense in inconveniencing the visiting azalea-admirers. Somebody might get bit.

Hope wanted to make a statement while a large audience was present to appreciate the gesture. She laid plans and assigned roles. Three of her closest friends and associates, Arthur, Joan and Maddy, agreed to participate in what Hope referred to as "Operation Bark in the Dark!" She considered it the equivalent of Lincoln's Emancipation Proclamation for our furry friends.

Hope dipped into the ARF! treasury and ordered four industrial strength bolt cutters from a supplier in Jacksonville to be delivered the day of the scheduled doggie jail break. She also bought four Halloween-style animal costumes with stylized poodle masks from a local theatrical supply shop. The plan in its simplest form was to dress up as dogs, break into the animal shelter when everything was dark, cut the padlocks on all the cages, swing wide the doors, and set loose the inmates. Then escape out the back door while chaos ensued up front. What could possibly go wrong?

As it turned out, five things, actually. In the first place, the animal shelter was protected by an alarm system. Hope had done her homework. She located and bribed a former employee who provided her with the six-digit numeric combination to silence the alarm. Presuming the powers that be didn't change the code frequently it seemed like a good investment of funds. He also gave Hope a spare key to the front door which was a good thing because the keypad used to disarm the alarm system was inside the animal shelter. Hope didn't want to damage any more property than was absolutely necessary. She figured if they got caught at least there would be a minimum of Breaking if they were charged with Breaking and Entering.

In the second place the New Hanover County Animal Control facility was a division of the Sheriff's Office and, as such, was patrolled every hour on the hour by armed deputies. Not a problem. Hope figured they could be in and out in twenty minutes, leaving plenty of time to make a clean getaway.

In the third place, two of the bolt cutters were not industrial strength as ordered. They weren't strong enough to cut through wet cardboard. Based on a surf through the web that showed the interior of the animal shelter, the padlocks on the cages appeared to be sturdy. Consequently, Hope was obliged to divide the tasks up into subtasks between lock cutters (Hope and Joan) and cage clearers (Arthur and Maddy). The division of labor added a good five minutes to the mischief at hand, but they were still well within the time frame allotted to the project.

In the fourth place, not all the animals wanted their freedom. For whatever reason some of them cowered in corners and had to be coaxed to escape.

But fifth place was the showstopper. Not everybody was as committed to the cause as Hope.

The spare key worked a treat. Hope slipped the key into the lock and twisted it smoothly in a counterclockwise direction. The door didn't so much as squeak when it was opened. Arthur had brought along a shielded flashlight which he switched on. It was dark inside the animal shelter except for a dim light in the rear where the animals were caged. A blinking red light on the wall next to the door revealed the location of the alarm box keypad. Hope punched in the alarm code and the blinking red light turned green.

They tiptoed out to where the caged animals were kept and switched on the overhead lights. Apparently, the animals weren't used to being awakened in the dead of night because they set up a barking, growling and yipping frenzy that shook the rafters. The uniformed driver of a passing patrol car, a sheriff's deputy named Sherman Arundel, noticed the lights, heard the ruckus and pulled into the parking lot. Gun drawn, he approached the building and eased open the unlocked front door.

"Who's there?" he demanded.

Arthur and Maddy sprinted for the rear door. Joan tossed her bolt cutter to Hope and followed in their wake. The bolt cutter glanced off the concrete floor and smacked Hope on the leg, knocking her off balance just as she successfully sliced through the padlock on the first cage. The cage door swung open as Officer Arundel entered the back room. Officer Arundel was beset by a stampede of fleeing animals. He fell back on his heels, but he had the presence of mind to keep his pistol trained on Hope's right eyeball. She surrendered without a whimper.

Officer Arundel took Hope into custody and drove her downtown to be booked. One thing led to another. Hope finally ended up in the New Hanover County Detention Facility to await trial. She was duly convicted of breaking and entering, contributing to public nuisance, property damage, assaulting an officer of the law and a variety of other minor offenses and was sentenced to six months behind bars. Fortunately, all her misdeeds were classified as misdemeanors. She was remanded to the New Hanover Correctional Center where she met May Ruth Armstrong.

May Ruth was doing time for busting another lady's nose in a bar fight. The other lady happened to be the daughter of a judge who lived at Landfall. May Ruth never was very good at choosing whose nose she broke.

Hope and May Ruth became fast friends. For Hope it was purely a practical decision. Hope realized she needed protection from the other inmates. May Ruth represented the answer to the question of her own personal safety while she was inside. May Ruth liked the cut of Hope's jib.

They were released within three weeks of each other and moved in together. It was okay since neither of them was a convicted felon. Hope wanted to finish her business degree at UNCW. May Ruth had big plans for starting a business of her own. She'd been an avid web surfer while she was inside. Now she knew enough of the technical details to be able to set up and operate her own personal Meth Lab.

They discussed the huge profit potential for the enterprise. They even found an abandoned shack in Whiteville, down the road from Wilmington, they could use for their base of operations. May Ruth would be responsible for production and distribution. Hope could handle the business issues. It was a marriage made in heaven. Well, made in the New Hanover Correction Center to be precise. But they both knew it was gonna make them rich as Croesus. Whoever that dude used to be.

Burner Phone

Herman Periwinkle was an accountant by trade and a humanitarian by nature. He was also an avowed pacifist and a happily married man. Most of the time anyhow. He and his wife, Margaret, had engaged in a bit of a tiff that Friday morning and Herman was going to be a few minutes late for work.

The tiff had to do with bacon. Margaret (he refused to call her Peg) cooked bacon for Herman's breakfast at least once a week, but today it didn't look like bacon.

"It's turkey bacon," explained Margaret patiently. "It's much healthier for you than those pork-based products."

"You can't get bacon from a turkey," groused Herman. "Bacon comes from pigs."

To punctuate his astute observation, he stood abruptly and hurled his napkin on the table. In standing, Herman's left knee joggled a loose leg on the kitchen table (Herman was not Mr. Handyman Around the House!), upsetting a water glass and dousing his trousers. Margaret was aghast. Herman was obliged to return to his bedroom and change into another suit. When he returned to the kitchen Margaret was collecting the dirty dishes from the table.

"I think I'll go spend the weekend at Mother's," she said quietly. "I think you need a little time to yourself."

As it was a warm mid-May morning, the air fresh and clean, Herman decided to walk the ten odd blocks to work. He needed the exercise and, after his brief confrontation with Margaret, he surely needed to clear his head.

While he was certain his underlings wouldn't mind his tardiness, Herman was a stickler for punctuality. Furthermore, aside from his uncharacteristically churlish outburst this morning, he positively detested incivility. Which is why the disheveled girl leaning against a lamppost on the corner caught his eye. It was 8:15 in the morning and the poor girl appeared, to put it politely, inebriated in the extreme. Furthermore, one of her ample breasts was hanging out! Well, not yet fully liberated from her eviscerated bra, but certainly in peril of imminent exposure. Which is why in passing Herman tipped his hat and said, "May I be of service, Madam?"

Who knew such an innocent interjection could've turned Herman's tidy life upside down! Upon closer inspection he could see she'd been crying.

"Fucker ripped my shit, rode me down in the elevator and threw my sorry ass out the door," she sobbed. "I got nowhere to go, Daddy."

Herman removed the neatly folded white handkerchief from the breast pocket of his suit and handed it to the girl. She blew her nose and stuffed the soiled hanky in the lefthand cup of her shredded bra, along with the bulk of her partially dangling breast.

"Thanks for the sympathy," she sniffed, extending her hand. "Kourtney Madison. What's your name?"

"Herman Periwinkle," said Herman, firmly grasping Kourtney's damp hand. "How can I help?"

Kourtney launched into a litany of epithets regarding the afore-mentioned Fucker, a scoundrel whose birth name was David Pelham, and whose parentage was of questionable legitimacy.

"So, he dumped me in the street without so much as a kiss on the cheek or a fare thee well," Kourtney wailed. "The rest of my clothes are still hanging up there in his closet. He like to ripped off the clothes I got on. I did not steal his fucking credit card. I swear to God!"

Herman took pity on the unfortunate waif and her plight. Well, it wasn't only that. A nipple had winked at him while the maiden was stuffing the recalcitrant breast back into the confines of her tattered bra. Herman wasn't proud if it but there it was. Herman was hooked.

"Let me see if I can rectify the situation," said Herman, pulling out his cellphone.

He dialed a number and waited.

"Peter? It's Herman. Are any of your suites vacant at the moment? It's urgent."

"Herman, my man," laughed Peter. "Don't tell me Peggy finally kicked your stuffy ass out!"

"Your sister has no earthly reason to kick me out," replied Herman indignantly. "A friend of ours has become homeless through no fault of her own. She needs a place to stay for perhaps a week. I'd appreciate it if you didn't mention our charitable endeavor to Margaret. She might not understand. The charity, I mean."

"Bill it to the company as usual?" chuckled Peter. "And my lips are sealed."

"We shall consider her a visiting executive in residence," agreed Herman. "Her name is Kourtney. Um, what was your last name again, dear?"

"Madison," replied Kourtney. "It's Kourtney Madison."

"Did you get that, Peter? I'll bring her over now."

Herman disconnected and called one of his associates.

"Darrel? Herman. I'll be a bit late coming in this morning. We've had an important client fly in for the weekend. I'm getting her settled at Hammond House. I'll be there as soon as I can manage."

He disconnected.

"You must be some hot shit, Herman," smiled Kourtney. "I'm impressed."

"I do have a measure of influence within my jurisdiction," sniffed Herman. "Shall we go? There's a dress shop on the way. We need to get you cleaned up."

They stopped in at the Chic Boutique where Kourtney visited the ladies' room, washed her face, came back out and tried on several fashionable frocks before settling on a blue and white number that fit too tightly with a neckline that dipped too deeply for Herman's taste, but she did look more presentable. She also picked out a pair of comfortable shoes and a purple purse. Herman paid for everything with his company American Express card. In for a penny in for a pound. Even Herman had to admit Kourtney cleaned up nice.

They walked the remaining three blocks to Hammond House, which was right on the way to Herman's office. The company had chosen Hammond House to accommodate visiting firemen in large part because of its close proximity to their headquarters. The fact that Herman's brother-in-law ran the place did not play a major role in the decision.

Herman introduced Kourtney to the Hammond House crew. They were gracious, she was reciprocally delightful and Eldon, the desk clerk, nearly swallowed his tongue when Kourtney bent over to sign the guest register.

Herman escorted Kourtney to her suite. He opened the door, handed her the card key, and ushered her into the living room.

"Coffee maker is on the kitchen counter," said Herman. "Soft drinks are in the refrigerator. Instructions for operating the television set are on the desk in the foyer. I think you'll be comfortable here. I've got to be getting back to work."

"Can't you stay five minutes more, Hermie," asked Kourtney, reaching back and unzipping the frock. "I'd like to thank you for being so generous."

"I'm afraid I don't know what you have in mind, young lady," sputtered Herman. "I'm a happily married man."

"Not trying to bust up your marriage, Hermie," said Kourtney sweetly, slipping out of the frock entirely. She was down to her tattered bra and lace panties. "Did you know the ancient Greeks believed the Olympian God, Hermes, was a divine trickster? I'll bet you could show me a trick or two."

"I am not a trickster in any sense of the word," admitted Herman gloomily, sinking down on the beige sofa. "In fact, truth be told I'm not even certain about my ability to satisfy a woman. Not in that way, anyhow."

"Do I have a surprise for you, Hermie!" said Kourtney, unfastening her tattered bra. "I'm a squealer. When I climax, I make these little yipping noises. When you make me come, you'll know it, sweetie! Loud and clear. You wanna try?"

It turned out he did, and they did, and she did. True to her word, Kourtney yipped frequently and fervently. Herman was happier than he'd been in ages. He dressed, dropped three fifties on the nightstand in case Kourtney needed to buy food and stuff, strolled downstairs and whistled a nameless tune all the rest of the walk to work. What a lovely way to start the day.

After Herman left for work, Kourtney showered, put on her panties and bra, flopped back down on the bed, and dialed her soulmate, Frog, on the room phone. Frog, real name of Willie Jefferson, was also Kourtney's connection for weed. Frog lived in a one-bedroom apartment in Section 8 housing. Several years back, Frog was treated to an orchiectomy (castrated) when he tried to take over another dealer's territory. Frog and Kourtney had never successfully engaged in the sex act. They tried once and it was a disaster. Frog said it was like trying to whip a wildcat with a wet noodle. Karma-induced ED is a bitch.

"Hey Frog, I been relocated," Kourtney said. "David booted my pretty little ass out the door."

She proceeded to relate the details of her unwarranted dismissal and her subsequent rescue by Herman, who now had a spring in his step and a song in his heart.

"Dude loves me," she said. "I got dipped in shit, come out smelling like a rose. I was obliged to leave my stash behind. Would you be cool making a herb delivery to Hammond House? Suite 237. Normal rates apply."

"You in the market for some white lady?" Frog asked. "On special this week."

"Not sure my man is up to doing lines," said Kourtney. "Hermie ain't no David. Got to take him slow. We just barely got past the infidelity shit. I don't think he's ready for 'E' either. I'll let you know when we need the Skittles truck to come by. I will say this. When David introduced my ass to nose candy, shit changed my perspective about the intensity of a woman's clench when she's doing the bad nasty. Lordy, lordy. You need directions to Hammond House?"

"Not necessary, Babe," said Frog. "Me and Peter, we got an understanding."

"You what?" asked an astonished Kourtney. "I would've thought Hammond House was way out of your league."

"Don't sell me short, girl. When Peter entertain clients, they come here from places got way different attitudes. Medical marijuana be legal in most states these days. Recreational not far behind. Stand to reason some of his guest like to fire up a pipe of an evening. Frog be the man who fill the pipe. Careful though. No smoking in the room. Balcony be okay. Dude got rules about shit like that. Peter be cool long as you respect his rules."

Herman called Kourtney on the room phone at 11:00 Saturday morning.

"Good morning, sweetheart, hope I didn't wake you."

"Not at all, Hermie," yawned Kourtney. "I was just getting up. I need me some coffee."

"I have a surprise for you. Well, for us. Can I come over?"

"Hope you don't mind me naked. I rinsed out my new frock last night. It isn't dry yet. I don't have anything else to wear. All my clothes are still at David's."

"That's another thing. I thought I might take you shopping. At Nordstrom."

"Come on over then. A girl always likes to shop."

When Herman got to Suite 237, he knocked loudly on the door. He could hear a hair dryer going full blast somewhere inside the room. He waited and knocked again. The noise from the hair dryer ceased abruptly. Through the peephole he saw an eye looking back at him. Then the door opened. It was Kourtney. It was nothing but Kourtney.

"May I come in?" Herman asked shyly.

"You ask me that when I'm standing here buck-assed naked?" grinned Kourtney. "You sure damn can, and I'd say you're way overdressed."

Herman had a plastic shopping bag in his hand. He came gingerly into the room. God, she was gorgeous. He put the bag on the rumpled bed.

"I bought us Burner Phones," he stammered. "Things went so well yesterday I thought we should have a way to communicate in private. I hope you don't think I'm taking too much for granted."

"That's sweet of you, Hermie," said Kourtney, sitting on the bed and opening the bag. "I left my iPhone at David's along with the rest of my life."

"They're Androids," said Herman. "I didn't know you had an iPhone. Sorry. Androids were a thousand bucks cheaper. I can take them back if you wish."

"Not a problem," said Kourtney. "My iPhone is backed up in the iCloud. I can restore my contacts and photos from the backup. I don't need anything else. Come over here and sit down so I can thank you."

After her appreciation had been fully expressed, along with a jubilee of yips and squeals, Kourtney went into the bathroom to dress while Herman recovered his composure face down on the bed. This new regimen of sexual calisthenics was gonna take some getting used to. Herman only hoped his heart was up to the task.

Shopping at Nordstrom was somewhat more expensive than Herman had anticipated. Not a problem. Herman had a savings account he kept in case of emergencies. This was as close to an emergency as Herman ever hoped to come.

At home that night Herman tried out the new Burner Phone. He sent a lurid text to Kourtney. She responded in what can only be described as four-letter-word, flagrant sexting. She attached a selfie and a video. Herman watched the video four times before going to bed. Margaret was coming home tomorrow afternoon. He wondered if he might have time for one more shot of morning sunshine before she arrived. He sure hoped so. Fun time with Kourtney was becoming dangerously addictive.

Peter normally took Sundays off but this Sunday he decided to come in and balance the books. Besides he wanted to check out the new girl, Kourtney. Apparently that rascal Herman was surreptitiously inclined to frolic in the depths of depravity. Jesus! The girl was young enough to be his daughter. Well, whatever floats your boat. Peter knew his sister wasn't exactly your traditional poster girl for Erogenous Zones Incarnate. At least she'd always seemed like a bit of a prude. Peter waited until 10:30. Then he phoned room 237.

"Ms. Madison? Peter Alexander here. I hope you're enjoying our hospitality."

"Good morning, Peter," replied Kourtney. "I was just thinking of you. If you have a few spare minutes, I'd like to discuss an arrangement we might find mutually beneficial. Can you come up?"

Peter disconnected and hurried upstairs to 237. Kourtney was waiting beside the open door.

"Come on in," said Kourtney with a smile. "I believe we have an acquaintance in common. A Mr. Willie Jefferson?"

"Is this an attempt at extortion?" asked Peter, frowning. "I must warn you in advance, I'm not an easy man to hornswoggle."

"I don't have hornswoggling on my agenda," said Kourtney. "In fact, hornswoggling's the furthest thing from my mind. What you're doing with Frog is your business. I'm suitably impressed by your enterprising attitude, however. I merely suggest that you and I may have a mutually profitable opportunity to provide an additional value-added menu item for your clients as well as for ourselves. Interested?"

"Intrigued," said Peter, coming into the room and closing the door. "Details?"

Kourtney laid it all on the line. How she'd been kicked out by her Sugar Daddy. How she had no visible means of support. How Herman had saved her out of the goodness of his heart. And how Peter had so kindly taken her in. Now she had an idea as to how she might repay his kindness.

"I'm not all that familiar with fancy hotel chains but I've always imagined the concierge had a list of services a regular customer might ask for. Services pertaining to restaurants, theater, entertainment, companionship, things of that sort. I thought we might bring the companionship service in house, so to speak."

"I see where this is leading, and I'm not opposed to providing an additional level of service to our clients," said Peter. "But how do I know you can perform?"

"I don't expect you to flog a product before you sample the goods," said Kourtney with a smile, unbuttoning her new Nordstrom blouse. "Have you ever made a woman squeal?"

Well, Peter had to admit he had not. Although to be perfectly honest, Peter suspected he would never be able to make that statement again!

After Peter left the room Kourtney got a text from Herman.

"Miss you. Margaret is on her way from New Bern. ETA around 5:00. Any chance for a quickie before she comes?"

"Only if I can come too. I love to come with you. Hurry over."

And it was true. Kourtney really liked the fussy old fart. In her way.

After Herman left, his face wreathed in smiles, Felice, the little Hispanic maid, dropped by to clean the room. She shyly mentioned to Kourtney that Peter had told her everything and did that mean Kourtney was now a full-fledged member of the team? Kourtney said sure was, wanna dance? Felice did wanna and what a delightful dance it was. Kourtney was rapidly ingratiating herself with the help. She loved her new role.

On Monday morning David Pelham phoned Frog.

"Frog? It's David. When she left on Friday, Kourtney neglected to take her clothes and her toys. I wondered if you had a phone number I could call so she could Uber over and get her stuff."

Frog gave David the number of Hammond House. David called and asked for Kourtney. Kourtney answered on the second ring.

"I feel really bad about Friday," said David. "There's no excuse for my behavior. I came across my missing credit card in an old pair of pants. I don't expect you to forgive me. I packed your toys and clothes in a big suitcase. You can come over and get it whenever you wish."

"This afternoon around 2:00 works for me," said Kourtney softly. "I'm sorry too, David. I thought we had something special going on. But we both know once the trust is gone you can never get it back."

Kourtney hung up and called Frog.

"Frog? Kourtney. I need a ride to David's at 2:00. Love you forever."

"Not a problem, Babe. Love you forever back. See you soon."

They got to David's apartment building at 1:45. Kourtney was dressed in her new blue and white frock. She carried her purple purse. Kourtney felt strangely liberated.

"Wait here by the curb," she told Frog. "Keep the motor running. This won't take long."

She went inside the red-brick, high-rise apartment building and took the elevator to the twelfth floor. Walked down the hall to unit 1207. Knocked on the door and waited. David opened the door. Behind David she could see her suitcase, wide open on the floor in the middle of the living room. It was filled with clothes and toys. David looked like he'd been crying.

"I don't want you to go," he sobbed. "I love you."

"You gave me no choice when you spiked my drink and threw me out," said Kourtney, coming into the living room. "I already have a new life. Without you in it."

David closed the door.

"Can't we talk about this?" he pleaded.

"Fuck you, David," said Kourtney softly. "And the horse you rode in on."

David whirled Kourtney around and punched her full in the face. She dropped like a sack of spuds. David grabbed the purple purse and began rummaging around in it. He found the Burner Phone. It was locked. He remembered Kourtney had a five-year-old daughter. What was her birthday? MMDDYY. David plugged it in. The phone unlocked. David scrolled to Kourtney's texts. There was one active thread. Hermie.

David opened the sliding glass door and went out onto the terrace. It was mercifully quiet for a Monday afternoon. Very little traffic on the street below. David read the erotic textual exchanges between Kourtney and Hermie. Disgusting. This Hermie guy was a married man. David phoned Hermie's number.

"Is this Hermie?' David shouted. "You stole my girl, you son of a bitch, I'm ratting you out to Margaret. I bet she'll fuck you over good. Asshole!"

Kourtney shook her head. There was a ringing in her ears. She could hear David out on the terrace, mumbling to himself. Her purple purse was on the floor, its contents strewn all over the carpet. She stumbled to her feet. She heard the words, "Is this Hermie?" She bent over like a defensive lineman, aimed straight for David's solar plexus. She hit him full force at the word "Asshole!" The Burner Phone flew from his grasp and landed face up on the living room carpet. David didn't fare nearly so well. He hit the railing on the terrace and tumbled over. A twelve-story drop is a hundred and fifty feet. Unfortunately, David had never learned to fly. He hit with a lugubrious splat on the pavement below.

"Incoming," Kourtney hollered as she ran back into the apartment.

She grabbed the Burner Phone, stuffed her things back in the purple purse, closed the suitcase and sprinted for the door, hurried down the hall to the elevator where she hit the Down button. Fortunately, the elevator was still waiting at the twelfth floor. The doors whispered open. She punched the first-floor button, the doors whispered shut, and the elevator descended to the lobby.

She threw her suitcase in Frog's backseat and jumped in front.

"Go, go, go," she urged, and they sped off into the waning afternoon.

When Herman received the phone call from David, he snapped out of his testosterone-driven trance. For the first time since Friday, he fully appreciated the matrimonial consequences of his momentary lapse in judgment. He went home that night after work and related the whole sordid tale to Margaret, omitting a few eloquent yips. Margaret was in a merciful mood. She'd forgotten what it was like, living with her mother. She would forgive Herman for his dastardly misdeeds in exchange for a promise on the spot that he would henceforth mend his wicked ways. Herman readily agreed to her distaff proposition. As he held Margaret safe in his arms, visions of the delectable Kourtney danced in his mind; a fade-to-black fantasy of erstwhile erotic pleasure, and he wondered briefly if Kourtney could possibly be persuaded to teach Margaret how to squeal.

May Ruth Pays the Price

Five months had passed since Hope and May Ruth were released from the New Hanover County Correction Center. Hope had seamlessly resumed her role as fulltime student at UNCW, parttime escort, and mostly absentee mother of her baby daughter, Faith, and was two months shy of graduating Magna Cum Laude (her sex worker associate, Addie, the other member of the female contingent that comprised the infamous *Ménage à Trois* package, referred to it as graduating Magnum Come Loudly!) with a bachelor's degree in Business Administration.

May Ruth was busily fine tuning her skills as an amateur purveyor of the Meth variety of pharmaceutical dreams. They'd leased and gussied up the dilapidated shack in Whiteville. Curtains on the windows, rugs on the floor. A wood stove for cooking product. An industrial strength ventilation system to waft away the fumes. Storage shelves from IKEA. Things were proceeding according to plan.

"What exactly is the plan?" asked Hope over breakfast one Saturday morning. "Here I am a full, albeit silent, partner in the business and I don't even know what the business is."

"We cook up Meth, package it and sell it," said May Ruth around bites of country ham. "I didn't know you were such a good cook."

"For starters, what's Meth?" asked Hope. "I know that sounds dumb, but I've never grasped the whole concept. I mean I get Ecstasy and Coke. Grass too. Meth not so much."

"Meth is short for Methamphetamines," said May Ruth. "You want the whole chapter and verse?"

"Dish, May Ruth," said Hope. "Pretend I'm a Venture Capitalist and I'm interested in investing in your company."

"Your traditional street grade crystal meth is made from ephedrine and pseudoephedrine, both produced by legitimate chemical companies," she continued. "Medical methamphetamines have been used by doctors for centuries to treat a variety of ailments. Meth stimulates the central nervous system. The Controlled Substances Act of 1970 defined meth as a Schedule II drug which means the DEA recognizes that meth has some limited benefit but it's still dangerous. And it's addictive as a motherfucker."

"So far so good," said Hope. "How does one go about producing this evil substance?"

"If one is a huge pharmaceutical company, one produces meth in a factory-like environment, complete with standards that adhere to OSHA specifications," replied May Ruth pedantically. "If one is a dirtbag such as me and thee, one makes crystal meth by boiling down a compound that contains ephedrine and pseudoephedrine, drying it out and selling it by the gram. Examples of such compounds are over-the-counter cold medicines and weight control pills. The tradename Sudafed is shorthand for pseudoephedrine. You may recall they stopped selling Sudafed in its original form in 2006 when President Bush signed into law The Patriot Act which contained provisions of the Combat Methamphetamine Epidemic Act."

"Whoa, May Ruth!" teased Hope. "You sure do know your shit! And here I thought you was just a plain old garden variety high school dropout."

"Fuck you, girlfriend," sniffed May Ruth. "And the school bus you rode in on."

"Anyhow isn't it dangerous to boil down the basic ingredients," asked Hope. "I think I read that somewhere."

"That's definitely one of the issues," admitted May Ruth. "The solvent most frequently used in the reduction process is gasoline. Gas has been known to explode when it comes in contact with flame. Then there's the fumes. Shit will mess with your lungs if you breathe too much. And then there's the Feds who go out hunting meth labs. That's why we hung chintz curtains on all the windows. To keep out the snoopers. Sometimes they got drug sniffing dogs. Cooking crystal meth gives off a distinctive odor. Heavy on the stink! Dogs can smell it for miles around."

"And here I thought it was all fun and games and profit," said Hope. "Tell me again why we're doing all this?"

"Cause we're gonna be richer than Croesus," laughed May Ruth. "Whoever the fuck he was."

Hope graduated on the following Saturday. She did not attend the ceremonies as she and Addie had a *Ménage à Trois* session scheduled for 2:30 in the afternoon with Charlie Easterman. Charlie's wife had taken the kids to visit her sister in Knoxville, Tennessee. Charlie wanted to linger after the hour was over. He had nowhere better he wanted to be. Addie shooed him out the door.

On Monday May Ruth started cooking crystal meth. She had a pusher lined up down by the Riverwalk who needed product and was willing to pay extra if it was ready by 7:30

that night. May Ruth got careless, a pot tipped over and the meth lab blew sky high. They never found her body. A careful examination of the lease papers produced the names of the two partners.

Federal agents visited the home of Hope Kennedy and May Ruth Armstrong on Wednesday morning around 11:00. Hope was still mourning the loss of her friend. The Feds asked Hope if she had an attorney to represent her. She admitted she did not but that she had a friend who might know someone. The Feds sat down on the sofa to wait.

Charlie Easterman had given Hope his business card. Hope called Charlie at the bank.

"Charlie," she said tearfully when the other end of the line was answered. "It's Bambi. I hate to bother you but I'm in a jam. Can you help?"

She briefly explained the situation to Charlie.

"Can you put one of the agents on the phone?" asked Charlie. "I'd like to speak with him."

Hope handed the phone to one of the agents who listened carefully, nodded his head, and disconnected the call. He handed the phone back to Hope.

"We're sorry for taking up so much of your time," he said gently. "Your friend on the phone was very helpful. He explained he had firsthand knowledge that you weren't part of the meth lab operation but that your roommate forged your name on the lease. He also referred me to a law firm in town that could provide further information if I found it necessary to pursue the issue. I'm satisfied that we have identified our culprit. She's dead. Therefore, we can consider the case closed. I do have one more question if I may."

Hoped nodded.

"Who's Bambi?"

Silent Witness

John Nichols was the best classical guitar player in Willow Glen. He was also quite possibly the best classical guitar player in the entire city of San Jose, California, or maybe even in all of Santa Clara County. He was pretty sure he wasn't the best classical guitar player in the State of California. There were a few classical guitar players down in Southern California who could strum John's socks off.

John played his six-string, classical guitar Friday evenings from 8:30 to 10:00 at the Three Sisters Bookery in The Pruneyard shopping center in Campbell where they sold baked goods and good books. He drew a respectable-sized crowd, mostly couples in their mid-fifties who'd been coming to listen to John for the past thirteen years. John kept a tip jar up on stage, nestled next to his wooden stool. He wasn't there for the tips, but he felt that contributing to his tip jar allowed his fans to participate more fully in the experience.

John's real job was working days as a Mainframe Systems Programmer for IBM down at the intersection of Monterey and Cottle Roads in San Jose. John knew he was a dinosaur. Most of his peers had either taken early retirement or had gone on to become webmasters in the brave new world of cloud computing. Mainframe Systems Programmers were a dying breed. The job paid well, though, and John wasn't sure he could convert his arcane skills to the new technology. Besides, he was a mere ten years away from retirement himself.

John had never married. It wasn't that he didn't find women attractive. Some of the women John dated were downright gorgeous. But John had never come across a woman who fit the bill. The long-term bill, that is. Weekends and trips to Tahoe were one thing but John was reluctant to share his space with another human being. Other human beings tended to be messy or fussy or cranky or a lethal combination of all three. On balance, one might say that John Nichols was a happy guy.

The third Friday in February didn't start out well. John got rear-ended on his way to work. The accident was caused by patchy fog, unusual for this time of year but not unheard of. By the time he and the other guy had exchanged insurance information and driver's licenses it was obvious that John was going to be a good fifteen minutes late for work anyhow, so he stopped on the way at a Panera Bread place for one of their egg souffles.

The breakfast crowd had thinned. John was the only patron in line. The lady behind the cash register was new. Her name tag read "Rita." Rita looked to be a comfortable forty, but she'd aged well. The top button on her taut uniform had unaccountably come loose. Nothing under her blouse looked forty. It looked lovely. In the spring a young man's fancy turns to you know what. You know what else? It isn't only in the spring, and it isn't only young men. It's every man's fancy from puberty to Alzheimer's and after Alzheimer's it only becomes slightly less focused. John tapped in his phone number.

"Mr. Nichols?" Rita smiled warmly, glancing at the screen on her cash register. "Which egg souffle may I get for you this morning?"

"Which ever one you think looks breast," stammered John. "Sorry, looks best."

"Breast works for me," she whispered softly. "I'll bring you one that's nice and firm. Do you want anything to go with it?"

"Coffee," he replied shakily.

"Cream?" she grinned, handing John the sensual souffle on a plastic tray.

"Are you free tonight?" rasped John, enthralled. "I'm playing classical guitar at the Three Sisters Bookery tonight. It's a bookstore at The Pruneyard. I'd love for you to come. I'll save you a front row seat."

"I'd love to come, John," she said, flashing a furtive peek at a perky nipple. "I'll sit in the front row, but I refuse to wear panties. That's $8.37 including tax."

John handed Rita a twenty with a trembling hand.

"Keep the change. See you tonight. You know how to get there?"

"I'll just follow the music. See you tonight, John."

John had a hard time keeping his mind on his work. The image of that elusive nipple teased him right up to lunchtime. He was tempted to go back to Panera Bread and have soup and a sandwich for lunch, but he was afraid Rita might not be there. Nor did he want to appear too eager. He didn't want to lose the upper hand. Dang she looked good enough to eat.

At 5:00 John clocked out. He had plenty of comp time on the books, so he didn't feel bad about putting in a leisurely seven hours instead of his usual ten. To be honest most of the seven hours had been spent in a fog. And the fog was named Rita.

John got to The Three Sisters Bookery at 7:30 to set up. Friday night guitar selections were performed in a section of the bookstore where they usually hosted author readings and book signings. The author podium had been replaced with a slightly raised, portable stage. John's favorite wooden stool with the tip jar nearby was positioned toward the front of the shallow stage. Three rows of folding chairs had been set up to accommodate the audience. John deftly hung a Reserved sign on the middle chair in the first row, just in case.

Tuning the guitar before a performance in February wasn't much of a chore. In the mid-summer heat, they sometimes held performances outside in the courtyard. The blazing heat of the day that lingered well into dusk raised havoc with the tension in the nylon guitar strings. But inside the bookstore, the strings were docile, compliant, subdued. John was anything but docile. He felt tense as a tightened nylon string.

For the evening's entertainment, John had chosen several selections from the Andrés Segovia songbook. In his early period Segovia performed mostly flamenco pieces. John was in an uncharacteristically flamboyant mood. Nonetheless he drew the line at bolo ties and silk shirts, let along those castanets and wicked dancing boots. He did opt for a Western outfit. A striped shirt with snaps down the front and faded blue denims. No Stetson though. John wasn't a hat guy.

At 8:15 the patrons of the art began wandering in. The Reserved sign on the folding chair in the middle seat of the front row drew furtive glances but the chair remained unoccupied even after the clock had struck 8:30. John began to play his signature opening number, "Sheep May Safely Graze" by Bach in the key of G.

At 8:37 a slight disturbance rippled through the hushed room. Rita delicately picked her way to the front row, tugged her tight, black leather skirt down and sat on the chair sporting the Reserved sign. Her white cashmere sweater didn't do a thing to mask the fact that she was braless. The damp chill outside had perked up her generous nipples. John was a hog for generous nipples. She spread her knees slightly and two pair of lips smiled up at John. John flubbed the ending chord for the first time in his illustrious career.

Andrés Segovia had never performed his songbook better. A fifteen-minute intermission at 9:30 allowed Rita to approach the stage and slip a ten-dollar bill inside John's tip jar.

"Are you enjoying the evening so far?" she asked.

"Immensely."

"If you don't have any plans for later, I know a place on Bascom," she said. "You'll have to drive. I took an Uber over, but I didn't schedule the return trip. There's a bar named First Impressions across the street from the light rail station. It's dark and smoky inside. I hope you don't mind dark and smoky places."

"Dark and smoky works for me," whispered John. "God you're gorgeous."

"I hope you like First Impressions," she murmured. "Sometimes they're the best kind."

At 10:00 on the dot John struck his final chord of the evening, stood and bowed to a smatter of applause from the dwindling crowd and stowed his instrument in its case. He stepped off the stage, Rita slipped her hand through his waiting arm and they sped off through the night to the bar named First Impressions.

The bar was everything John had hoped for, including almost empty. They sat at a table in the rear. A scantily clad waitress came over and put coasters on the table.

"Hi, Rita, the usual?"

"Hi Myrna, yes please. The drink that bears my name. Margarita on the rocks, no salt. And I believe the gentleman will have a Dos Equis. You're a beer drinker, right John?"

John nodded. The waitress departed.

"I loved the concert," Rita smiled, taking John's hand in hers. "You're incredibly talented. How long did it take you to master the guitar?"

"I've been playing since I was eleven. Not classical at first. At first, I wanted to be a rock star, but my parents wouldn't hear of it. They're way too conservative. Dad was an engineer at IBM. He retired ten years back. Love your sweater."

Rita pulled John's hand across the table and leaned into it gently. The cashmere felt soft. The firm flesh under the cashmere felt heavenly. The drinks came. John almost came as well.

"To a lovely evening," said Rita, releasing John's hand and raising her glass. "Let's make it last."

Rita was extremely well read and surprisingly articulate. It turned out she'd traveled all over the world, living in a small village in Italy for three months after she graduated from college with a degree in Romance Languages. She had a rich sense of humor, and she held her liquor well. She was on her third Margarita when suddenly her mood turned serious.

"Are both your folks still living?" she asked.

"Mom died three years ago," John said softly. "It was the cancer. Dad's healthy, but he misses her a lot. I try to see him on weekends. It's not always possible. I'm his only living relative."

"My own Dad passed on Wednesday," Rita said, dabbing at her eyes with a tissue. "He was a retired insurance executive living in Omaha. I can't afford to fly to Nebraska so I could attend the funeral on Monday. My older brother's executor of Dad's estate, but he won't send me the airfare. I promised to pay him back out of my share of the inheritance, but Franklin won't budge. He's a tight assed son of a bitch."

"I might be able to help out," said John. "Airfare to Omaha can't be too bad."

"Trying to book a seat this late in the game is awfully expensive," said Rita, shaking her head. "I called United after I got home from work. That's why I was late to your concert. The cheapest fare is $537 round trip. That's in coach. The plane leaves San Jose tomorrow morning at 11:00. They only had three seats left. I'd pay you back, of course. If you wouldn't mind me sleeping over at your place, you could drive me to the airport in the morning. It would mean the world to me, John."

Suddenly the front door banged open.

"Hey, cowboy, what're you doing with my wife?" barked a gruff, baritone voice. "I thought I'd find you here, Letitia."

The big man strode over to the table where John and Rita were sitting. Rita was furious. John was dumbfounded.

"You come along home now," the guy demanded.

"Get the fuck out of here, Roy," snarled Rita. "This ain't none of your business."

"I'm making it my business," said Roy, grabbing Rita by the arm and dragging her up out of her seat.

Roy frog walked Rita out the door into the foggy night. Suddenly there was a squeal of brakes and a loud crash. John rushed to the door. The San Jose light rail train stood on the tracks outside. The bodies of a man and a woman lay crumpled on the tracks. Police sirens wailed in the distance.

"Do you know what happened?" asked a passerby.

"I have no idea," said John, shaking his head. "I was about to head home myself. You have a nice night. Hear?"

Hope Loses Faith

The death of May Ruth hit Hope harder than she thought it would. It wasn't as if they were lovers or anything. But there was a shared intimacy that doesn't happen between casual acquaintances. Jail time together probably helped.

Hope cranked up her sex work. In addition to the occasional *Ménage à Trois* gigs with Addie she began advertising on her own as a body rub girl. For the uninitiated, a body rub is a massage performed by a scantily clad, uncertified amateur that results in a happy ending. Your conventional body rub promises absolutely no therapeutic value although it tends to be considerably more expensive than a massage delivered by a professional. Men are a gullible gender.

Hope never did start looking for a job that would utilize her degree in business. For one thing when you're pulling down $150 for half an hour's worth of rubbing and tugging it doesn't make sense to apply for an apprentice position that pays minimum wage. For another thing there's something about toiling diligently in a socially unacceptable profession that messes with a person's sense of self-worth. Let's face it. No mother worth her salt ever raised a daughter to jerk cocks. Hope was pretty sure an HR applicant-screener wouldn't see her as executive material.

Given the standing of Hope's professional assignations and aspirations it came as no surprise when Howard Goodall's parents rescinded Hope's maternal visiting privileges. Their lawyers had an order drawn up that depicted Hope as a person who regularly committed acts of moral turpitude, was furthermore an unfit mother, and was therefore considered a real and enduring threat to the emotional and physical stability of her daughter. They cited her stint behind bars, her ads on BackPage and the fact that she was, *Prima Facie*, a sodomite.

Most folks believe sodomy is a crime between males. Not so. The meaning of sodomy can be more broadly defined to include any sexual penetration aside from vaginal intercourse, including oral and anal sex, whether between two men or two women or a man and a woman. Yikes! So even though an act of sodomy is no longer a crime, even in the State of South Carolina, it can be used to cast aspersions on the moral character of an individual.

Shortly thereafter Hope's mom and grandfather were killed in an automobile crash. Again, not a surprise. Grandpa was a heavy drinker and her mom hated to drive. Hope didn't even go to the funeral as she had a busy day scheduled. Since Hope was the only surviving relative, she inherited the doublewide. She told Addie she had no plans to move back home to Burgaw. Those days were behind her.

The final straw was when Addie told Hope she was moving to Gainesville, FL, with her new boyfriend, Clayton Wordsworth, who had been a professor of Black History at UNCW. Clay had been offered a position at the University of Florida. Hope hadn't even known Addie and Clay were dating.

Thus began Hope's descent down the constricting rabbit hole of despair, despondence and controlled substance abuse. Her daily routine gradually morphed into a circular pattern of Whore, Score and Do it Some More.

She did have a considerable amount of discretionary income. The balance in her Wells Fargo savings account ballooned way beyond her old daily average balance of $175. She got rid of the banal bicycle and bought a Harley Davidson hog, complete with saddlebags and a purple helmet with scarlet flames. Hope fancied herself the quintessential bad ass girl on a bike. She even upgraded her old Motorola flip-phone to an iPhone 4.

She kept the apartment she'd shared with May Ruth to live in and plied her trade out of various sleazy hotels on Market Street. One of her favorites was known locally as the Daytime Dump Motel. She stayed there so often she considered herself a charter member of their Hooker Express program where she soon gained status as a Phrequent Philanderer. And she thought about suicide on a daily basis.

One rainy midnight in early November, Hope rode her Harley out to Carolina Beach and parked by the boardwalk. Consumed with self-loathing, she got buzzed on crystal meth and quietly contemplated her bleak existence. Suddenly she had an overwhelming, meth-based inspiration. She hopped back on her Harley and sped off into the night. Across Snow's Cut Bridge, straight north on Carolina Beach Road, continued onto College Road, and thence to the fabled agricultural community of Burgaw.

Hope parked her hog in front of the doublewide, fumbled for the key she kept on a silver chain around her neck, jammed it into the lock and threw open the door. The place was a fucking mess. Hope collapsed, fully clothed, on the sofa and drifted off into a fitful sleep. Her dreams were filled with images she thought at first came from the fiery explosion of the meth lab that killed May Ruth but upon closer examination she realized they represented the after glare from all those burning bridges she'd left behind.

When she came to the next morning a diminutive stranger was perched on a folding chair beside the sofa, holding Hope's hand. Hope blinked. It was Miss Higgins.

"How're you feeling, sweetheart," asked Miss Higgins softly. "I thought you were dead."

"Where did you come from," asked a bewildered Hope. "And how did you know I was here."

"I got a phone call from an unknown number at 1:30 this morning," said Miss Higgins. "Then the caller hung up. I figured somebody had butt-dialed me, but I Googled the phone number and came across a reference to a BackPage ad for somebody named Bambi. The facial image of Bambi's reflection in the mirror seemed familiar. I realized it was you. You've put on weight."

"It's been a rough year," muttered Hope groggily. "Do we have any coffee?"

"I'll make some," said Miss Higgins. "I trust Instant is okay. I found a jar in the cupboard."

Miss Higgins boiled a pot of water, mixed up the evil potion and came back to sit beside Hope. She handed Hope the coffee. Hope took a sip and gagged.

"Was there an expiration date on the label?" she rasped. "This shit is terrible."

"Something about beggars and choosers," replied Miss Higgins. "Tell me what's going on."

Hope related the whole story, from Pell Grants to jail time to meth labs to body rubs to Harleys to the doublewide. Miss Higgins was silent.

"Wow," she sighed. "I'd say you've had a rough time of it sweetheart. So, what's the plan for the future?"

"There is no plan for the future," said Hope. "I've about run out of future. If I see another naked male body, I swear to God I'll scream. My bank account is down to shit. I was half-hoping I'd run the Harley into a tree on my way back home. No such luck. You got any ideas?"

"In your BackPage ad you referenced body rubs," said Miss Higgins. "Do you derive any satisfaction out of providing a therapeutic service to people?"

"Body rubs are hardly therapeutic," scoffed Hope. "I presume you speak the language."

"That's not what I meant," said Miss Higgins thoughtfully. "I was thinking more along the lines of a legitimate, certified massage practitioner. I have a friend who runs a massage certification school in Leland. I've put a little aside in what I call the Miss Higgins Needy Scholarship Fund. I think you qualify."

"How long does the process take?" asked Hope. "I'm no longer the bright-eyed, gullible girl I used to be. And this chunky body's got a lot of miles on it."

"The program itself takes 635 hours of intensive study and hands-on training," said Miss Higgins. "I doubt if any of your prior Bambi experience would qualify as hands-on training. So, figure you do this forty hours a week. You could conceivably be certified three months after you're accepted. First though, we've got to do something about that body. Jesus! You look a mess."

"Come on, Miss Higgins," Hope teased. "You've got to at least admit I've grown me some tits."

"And we might consider dumping the Harley," said Miss Higgins. "It's a bit intimidating."

"The Harley stays," said Hope. "But I'm on board with the rest of the program. And may I say something seriously? I love you, Miss Higgins."

"I love you too, Hope," said Miss Higgins, giving Hope's shoulder a squeeze. "Now get out there and make us both proud!"

Tell Laura I Love Her

Laura Montaigne was the best goddamned certified real estate appraiser in Durham, North Carolina. For the past five years she'd worked for herself out of an office near the Southpoint Mall. Laura was thirty-seven years of age, single, sexually liberated, and proud of it. And she was a 3.5 tennis player, closing in on 4.0. Laura played tennis with her partner, Jacqueline Winston, three times per week, come rain or come shine. When it rained, the pair played on an indoor surface down the street in Chapel Hill.

Laura spent at least one weekend a month at the beach, usually in South Myrtle Beach, South Carolina. She owned a membership in a timeshare with footpath access to the Atlantic Ocean. The timeshare was part of a much larger association of timeshares so if Laura wanted to spend time in for instance, Las Vegas, she could use her points there.

Laura was also a big fan of theater. She had an annual subscription to the Durham Performing Arts Center (DPAC). DPAC plays host to several off-Broadway plays during the year. Laura was partial to musicals. She was particularly fond of Steven Sondheim plays.

Jackie and Laura had been best friends ever since Laura moved to Durham from Western North Carolina twenty years ago. Laura grew up in EarthFirst, an unincorporated, ecologically oriented community near Asheville. EarthFirst was dedicated to restoring the planet to its original pristine state. Laura left her EarthFirst chums and neighbors when she was awarded a four-year, academic scholarship to attend Duke University. She initially majored in philosophy but soon learned that there ain't no money in philosophy, so she switched her major to business.

Jackie, for her part, grew up surfing with the boys. Her parents, both deceased several years back, had been professors at UNCW in Wilmington. Jackie spent all her spare time near the ocean. When she was in high school, she volunteered to help out at the Sea Turtle Sanctuary in Topsail Beach, caring for loggerhead sea turtles during nesting season. The experience convinced her that she did not want to become a Marine Biologist. Although it's not politically correct to disrespect sea turtles, they're incredibly stupid creatures. They're afraid of everything. They can't even retract their heads and flippers into their shells like normal turtles. On the other hand, they've been around for a hundred and ten million years so they must be doing something right.

During Laura's freshman year, she and Jackie both enrolled in a class titled The Basis for Morality. The instructor was a randy grad student named Oscar Dolittle. The irony of the title was not lost on either student. The girls frequently hummed the theme to the Oscar Meyer Weiner commercial before class commenced. The entire class enjoyed the joke. Oscar did not. Both girls received 'D's for the course despite never having scored less than ninety-five on a test. Oscar said they flunked their orals. The girls protested that they'd never been given orals. Oscar replied that's precisely my point.

These days Jackie and Laura were members of the Durham Demolishers, a mixed gender team that competed around the state in tournaments. The others on the team were: Marty Sharp, a network security analyst; Dennis Rackham, a systems programmer at IBM; Donna Davenport, a paralegal and Barbara Letterman, a housewife and stay-at-home mom who lived in Apex.

So far this year the team was six and one in tournament play. The only tournament they lost was played the weekend Donna came down with the flu and her husband, Teddy, took her place. Teddy imagined himself a 3.5. He wasn't. At least it wasn't the Covid. Donna was back in action the next weekend, much to the other team members' relief.

Jackie owned her own Interior Design business, Winston Associates. Over the years, she'd handled her share of unwelcome attention from frisky husbands who had designs of their own on Jackie's slender, athletic frame. Thus far she'd managed to keep their testosterone-driven wiles at bay while she milked their wives' checkbooks. She enjoyed the harmless, flirtatious game. So far, she was up six Love.

Laura's phone rang. It was Jackie.

"Hey, Mountain Girl," said Jackie. "You ready for Hickory?"

"Hey, Beaches," replied Laura. "Got the Beamer gassed up and ready to rock and roll. How's the magical world of Bespoke Bullshit? You planning to drop by High Point on the way home?"

"Actually, I've always wanted to visit Grandfather Mountain," said Jackie. "I can't believe I've lived in North

Carolina almost forty years and never had the pleasure. You been there?"

"Asheville isn't that far from Linville," said Laura. "We used to go there every summer. The view from the Blue Ridge Parkway is spectacular. And the swinging bridge is scary as hell. Speaking of swinging, how's Marlon?"

"Marlon didn't make the cut. Gary's still on the roster, though. I need to hook you up one of these nights. Gary's got a roommate."

"I'll take a pass if you don't mind," laughed Laura. "Your hunky jock, Tony, didn't work out. A tad too touchy, feely for my taste. He was a good kisser, though. I give him full marks for tongue technique."

"Maybe you sent him packing before he got down to the good parts," said Jackie. "Just saying. Sometimes I think you expect way too much from a guy. They are the weaker gender, you know."

"See you at the VRBO Thursday night," said Laura. "Gotta dash. I'm doing an appraisal in Wake Forest at noon. Keep in touch."

Laura had worked as a real estate appraiser for fifteen years, shortly after she'd graduated from Duke. At first, she was an inhouse appraiser for a mortgage broker, but five years ago she bit the bullet and branched out on her own.

The money was good, and she was her own boss. She could do comps from her office but in order to perform a room-to-room inspection she had to visit the property. A typical on-site appraisal usually took two or three hours. Before she left home that Thursday morning, she'd packed an overnight bag and her tennis gear and stowed them in the trunk of her Melbourne Red Metallic 2018 BMW 320i. No sense going back to her place to change clothes. What she had on was comfortable enough for the three-hour drive to Hickory.

Barbara Letterman was responsible for keeping track of details regarding the team members' participation in the tournament. She'd sent out a group text on Tuesday. Laura and Jackie were competing in the 7.0 women's doubles. They were also competing individually in women's singles: Jackie in the 3.5 while Laura was playing up in the 4.0. Both Marty and Dennis were playing 3.5 men's singles. Dennis and Donna were teamed up in 7.0 mixed doubles. Everybody but Marty had matches scheduled for Friday, so they had to be in Hickory by Thursday evening at the latest. Marty was driving down Friday afternoon.

Individual matches were scheduled for morning, afternoon, and evening play, depending on the draw. It was all very complicated but that's one of the reasons Laura loved tournament play. She and Jackie were scheduled to play their first women's doubles match on Friday afternoon at 10:00 am. Jackie had her first singles match at 1:30 and Laura's first singles match was set to kick off around 5:30 Friday evening, depending of course on how the preceding matches went. Matches could last anywhere from forty-five minutes to as much as an hour and a half. You practically needed a mainframe computer to keep track of who was playing whom and when.

Doubles championship matches were played on Saturday, singles semifinal and championship matches were played on Sunday. It was a fact of life that not everybody hung around for the Sunday championship matches. Some people had a life outside tennis.

Barbara was treasurer for the team as well. She collected money from each member to cover out-of-pocket costs for the weekend trips when the tournaments were held out of town (lodging, shared meals and snacks, tournament fees if any). She also handled logistics for the trips. Her husband, Bruce, liked it that way. He wanted to make sure Barbara didn't book a place where she had to share a room. Not that Bruce didn't trust Barbara, but he had rules. For example, Barbara wasn't allowed to play doubles with an unmarried man as her partner. Married men were okay. Bruce figured their wives would put a stop to any hanky-panky, but you flat out couldn't trust men who weren't married. Bruce knew. He'd been an unmarried man himself.

For this weekend trip Barbara had booked a house through VRBO. The house was right on Lake Hickory. It was a six bedroom, five bath, 4900 square foot mini mansion that rented for $675 a night and slept fourteen people comfortably. Or six people if each guest wanted their own room. Seven if a spouse came along. Teddy came along with Donna sometimes. Bruce never came with Barbara. He trusted her to do the right thing. Marty was divorced and Bruce suspected Dennis was gay. In fact, if Barbara wanted Dennis to be her mixed doubles partner that was fine with Bruce. After all it was the twenty-first century.

What Bruce didn't know was that Marty had been hitting on Barbara for years, even before his divorce was final. Barbara didn't mind. She liked the extra-curricular attention. Things never got out of hand and even if they did Marty had had a vasectomy. Barbara always made sure Marty's room was right down the hall from hers. Just in case.

Laura got to the VRBO house at 6:07. Her BMW GPS plotted a precise course based on the address Barbara had texted her. Laura never ceased to be amazed by those devices. How could anybody know where everything was? It was a miracle. Barbara was waiting on the porch.

"Hey, you, how was the trip?" asked Barbara, getting up and giving Laura a hug.

"Uneventful, thanks to your implicit instructions," said Laura. "I didn't think the Wake Forest appraisal was ever going to end. The owner was late getting there, and the building inspector never did show up. I can get his report later. How are Bruce and the girls?"

"You know teenagers," said Barbara. "Thank God they can take care of themselves. Bruce is never around since they made him a senior partner in the law firm."

"Anybody else here yet?"

"Nope, just us chickens. Let's go inside. I'll show you your room."

Barbara allocated sleeping spaces. The team had an unwritten rule. If anybody had a problem with the room they were assigned it was best left unspoken, lest the discontented member be nominated to allocate the rooms the next time. Barbara was always fair though. The best rooms were never doled out to the same parties twice in a row. Laura had a broom closet the last time they were in Charlotte. She got the master suite this time.

"Nice place!" said Laura. "Must've cost an arm and a leg!"

"Your share is a little over $300 for the weekend," replied Barbara. "You can't even get a Motel Six in the Triangle for a hundred bucks a night. Come on out back. Let me show you the hot tub. Hope you packed your swimsuit."

"Sure damn did," said Laura, following Barbara through the kitchen. "I got the memo. And I love hot tubs!"

Dennis was next to arrive, followed shortly by Jackie, with Donna lagging close behind.

"I ordered us three large pizzas for dinner," said Barbara when they'd all assembled in the living room. "They should be here in fifteen minutes. That'll give you time to unpack your things. Marty won't be here till tomorrow afternoon. His loss."

There was a large picnic table on the lawn behind the house. They all sat around the table munching on pizza. Napkins and paper plates, no forks.

"Good idea," said Jackie between mouthfuls. "This pizza is delish."

"I don't know how you do it, Barbara," said Dennis. "You always plan the perfect weekend."

"It's a gift," smiled Barbara. "But the real gift is being allowed to spend my weekend with you guys instead of officiating an ongoing grudge match between a thirteen-year-old and a fifteen-year-old. Contrary to popular opinion, daughters are not sugar and spice and everything nice. Sometimes they're two-parts unrestrained emotion and one-part pure evil."

"If you guys don't mind, I'm gonna pass on the hot tub tonight," said Laura after the pizza was gone and the paper plates cleared. "Jackie and I have an early doubles match tomorrow morning. We'll need time to warm up before. That means I have to set my alarm for 6:00. Jackie, I'll knock on your door at 7:00. My suite has its own walk-in shower and a bidet. Eat your hearts out. Night all."

Laura and Jackie won their doubles match two and three. The entire match, including warmup, only lasted fifty-three-minutes. Jackie didn't even break a sweat.

"Piece of cake," grinned Jackie. "Let's get lunch. I'm starved."

Laura watched Jackie lose her singles match to a woman from Charlotte who, in Laura's opinion, should have been ranked much higher, 7:6(3) 6:4.

"I think I ran into a buzz saw," panted Jackie after shaking hands with the winner. "I need a nap."

Laura whipped her opponent from Charlotte soundly in straight sets, four and three.

"Let's go hop in the hot tub," said Laura. "All told we're dead even with the team from Charlotte."

"I need food first," whined Jackie. "It's almost 7:30 and I'm famished."

By the time they got back to the house it was 8:15. Barbara and Marty were sitting on the front porch, drinking wine.

"Dennis and Donna went to watch the Hickory Crawdads play the Asheville Tourists," said Marty. "They're both high-A minor league teams. Grab a couple wine glasses and join us. We were just doing a taste test on the Biltmore Estate's best Chardonnay. I picked up a chilled bottle at the Food Lion in Hickory before I got to the house. Yummy."

"I'll accept your kind offer of a glass of Chardonnay but only if I'm allowed to drink it in the hot tub," said Laura. "I'm all sweaty. I need to change into my bathing suit and relax."

"I'm with Laura," said Jackie. "I've already washed out of the tournament. I need to drown my sorrows."

"Don't forget the women's 7.0 doubles championship at noon tomorrow," said Laura. "We're still in the running!"

"You girls take the bottle," said Barbara with a smile. "Marty and I will sit out here for a while longer. It's such a lovely evening."

Laura and Jackie went to their rooms and changed. They met in the kitchen, fetched wine glasses from the cabinet and scampered out to the terrace where the hot tub was bubbling away. Barbara had warmed up the water in the hot tub. The temperature was perfect. They poured their glasses full of Chardonnay and stepped in.

"God this is great," sighed Laura, taking a sip of her wine. "I remember staying at the Biltmore Estate when I was a teenager. They hosted these ecological conferences every summer. My cousin, Jennifer, and I tagged along when we were thirteen. It was all very impressive. We were too young to drink wine, but the adults drank enough for all of us. It was a hoot."

"My parents were wine snobs," said Jackie, savoring her wine. "They refused to drink domestic wines. Not even wines from California. Mostly French but on occasion they would uncork a bottle of vintage Chianti."

"What did your folks teach?" asked Laura. "I know they were both professors, but I don't think you ever told me their specialties."

"Mom had her PhD in classical literature," said Jackie. "Her specialty was the Renaissance period. Petrarch, Boccaccio, those guys. Dad taught music theory at UNCW. He tutored budding young pianists on the side. Some of them were more budding than others."

"I'm not sure what you mean," said Laura, taking another swig of wine. "This stuff is really tasty."

"Mom caught him with his pants down one afternoon," said Jackie. "His student was only seventeen. Things were tense there for a while, but they eventually got past it. Or at least they pretended to."

"At least you knew who your Dad was," sniffed Laura, taking a gulp of wine and pouring another glass. "That's more than I can say."

"Come on, Mountain Girl," said Jackie, taking hold of Laura's free hand. "I thought you said you grew up in a commune. Everybody was one big happy family."

"That's what I thought too," said Laura softly. "Until the weekend at the Biltmore. Remember I told you about my cousin, Jennifer? Everybody always said we looked like sisters. Turns out her dad, my uncle Vern, had been sleeping with my mom and her mom both at the same time. Cedric, my dad, knew about it but he said it was all harmless fun. Mom and Aunt Fern were sisters, so it wasn't exactly incest.

But I'd say it was pretty fucked up. Not knowing who your real dad was, I mean. And the worst part was, everybody in EarthFirst knew about it but me."

"Jesus, sweetheart!" said Jackie. "No wonder you have trust issues."

"What do you mean?" asked Laura defensively, drawing back her hand. "Who says I have trust issues?"

"That's what Tony told Gary," said Jackie, taking hold of Laura's hand again. "Jesus Christ, don't shoot the messenger."

"Sorry, sweetheart, I didn't mean to bristle," said Laura, kissing Jackie on the cheek and getting up. "Maybe I do have trust issues after all. I'm going to bed. Love you, Beaches. See you in the morning."

Just past midnight Laura felt the bedsprings jiggle. Then Jackie snuggled up next to her and began fumbling with the string on her pajama bottoms. Laura snapped on the light and turned to face Jackie.

"I don't do girls," Laura hissed. "Get the fuck out of my bed."

"I thought you said," began Jackie. Then she slipped out of Laura's bed and walked slowly back to her own room.

The next morning Jackie was subdued at breakfast. Laura, on the other hand, was raring to go.

"Let's go kick some tennis ass, Beaches!" crowed Laura. "We got this thing!"

They didn't got this thing. Jackie played a lackluster game. Consequently, the girls lost in a third set tiebreaker 10:7.

"I'm off to Grandfather Mountain," said Jackie apologetically. "Sorry I fucked up. See you back at the ranch."

Laura won her singles match handily and was into the semifinals for Sunday. She slept like a baby. On Sunday she whipped her semifinals opponent and breezed into the championship, winning the match three and four. Marty approached her after the match.

"Did you hear about Jackie?" he asked. "She ran her car off the road on her way home from Grandfather Mountain. She died in the wreck."

Laura checked her phone. She had a message from Jackie. It was a group text to the team.

Tell Laura I love her

Laura put down the phone. She was surprised to find her eyes wet with tears. Then a phrase from an English Lit 101 class crept into her conscious mind. A couplet penned by an obscure American poet from the 60s.

For I was crying love me far too loud

To hear you whisper quietly I do.

Hope Abides

It was a beautiful morning in the lavish two-bedroom apartment on North Lumina Avenue, Wrightsville Beach in Wilmington, North Carolina. Well, morning is a relative term. The sun was already high in the sky. A casual glimpse of gently rolling ocean waves beyond the balcony outside the fourth floor sliding glass door showed them glistening in the glare. Alas, the playful school of dolphins had yet to make their appearance or perhaps they'd already departed to feed off Carolina Beach. Who doesn't love dolphins?

Hope Kennedy rolled over, stretched, and peeked groggily at the digital alarm clock on the nightstand. 11:30. Shit! Hope dragged herself out of the bed, taking care not to disturb Aretha Mae Jackson, the softly snoring lump on the California king size bed beside her (stage name Jaguar) and wandered into the master bathroom to prepare for the day.

Hope and Aretha Mae had been roommates going on four years now. The relationship had started out as a purely physical endeavor. After all, both ladies spent the bulk of their work hours catering to the whims of the masculine gender. It was only natural that they'd prefer to spend their leisure hours in the company of a kindred spirit. But over the four-year period they'd grown to like and respect each other. Believe it or not, once she had amassed sufficient funds in her passbook savings account at the College Road branch of Wells Fargo, Aretha Mae was determined to become a volunteer on Topsail Beach, intimately involved in the protection and preservation of sea turtles.

Aretha Mae was clever too. When Hope decided to have a few business cards printed up for her special clients, Aretha Mae came up with the layout. The text on Hope's private business card read:

A destitute dude may choke the chicken seven days a week

But Hope Beats Eternal

www.HopeAbides.com

The logo displayed in the top right-hand corner showed a ginger-haired, cartoonish character choking a scrawny chicken, its bright red tongue hanging out. The business cards were something of an underground legend throughout New Hanover County. Aretha Mae also had the bright idea for Hope's website, but it was Hope's favorite male client, Philip Applewhite, who did the actual implementation.

Philip Applewhite (that's Philip with one 'L' if you please and it's definitely not Phil!) was an accountant for KPMG, one of the larger accounting firms in the United States of America. These days, Philip worked out of his house in Hampstead. He'd been with Peat Marwick since before they merged with Klynveld Main Goerdeler and he still called it Peat Marwick when he was asked where he worked, sometimes adding "and Mitchell" for good measure. Old habits die hard. He was a Virgo by birth, a CPA by choice and a number cruncher by the grace of God. Philip didn't believe in astrology. Most Virgos don't. But he did believe in delivering a good day's work for a good day's pay. And he believed in the work Hope was doing.

Hope's chosen profession was admittedly beyond the conventional purview of socially acceptable and/or legitimate commercial occupations. She rented office space in a strip mall on Independence Boulevard. The neon sign in the window said, "Hope Kennedy, Certified Massage Therapist." She had a bookkeeper, a tax guy, and a scheduling service that booked her appointments. She did not have a receptionist or a waiting room. Clients were asked to park outside and wait for a text before they entered the establishment. Hope also had a degree in business from UNCW as well as her own LLC. Hope Kennedy was not your average hooker, thank you very much. Hope Kennedy was a dedicated professional sex worker.

Hope hopped out of the shower, dried off and got dressed in her best massage outfit du jour. Then she checked her texts from Theresa "Tess" Ceccino, the lady who scheduled her appointments. Oh God! The first session, a full hour, was set for 1:30. Hope barely had time for a quick bowl of cereal. Coffee first.

She popped a pod in her Keurig machine and browsed through the appointment list. Philip Applewhite was coming at 5:30. Hope chuckled at her own little private joke. She was pleased to see that Philip was due to drop by later in the day. Philip usually showed up sometime mid-afternoon during the rush. They barely had time to disrobe, do the bad nasty and get dressed again before her next client was due in the door.

Hope was a certified massage therapist who specialized in a variety of techniques related to the art of stress relief. She was fully qualified to provide her somewhat unconventional services to both men and women, although the vast majority of her clients were of the masculine persuasion. Hope was very good at what she did. Consequently, her grateful male clients usually left a little extra on the massage table. Most of them also left a token of their appreciation in Hope's tip jar.

A handful of carefully selected female clients were also treated to Hope's remarkable skills. In some ways Hope preferred servicing girls. They were easier to clean up after for one thing. And far less noisy at the finish.

Each of the first four appointments were half an hour long ($95 plus heart-felt gratuity), with fifteen minutes in between sessions for a quick shower, makeup repair and mouthwash. Then a full hour session at 4:00 ($145 plus charitable emolument) with a brief reprieve before it was Philip's turn in the barrel. The last client of the day, a newbie named Gregory DeSantis, was due in at 7:30 for a full hour. Hope was exhausted just thinking about the effort involved, but the revenue paid the rent.

At least most of today's clients were regulars. Hope hated the mating dance that went along with breaking in a new guy. How do you like it, hard or soft? Face down on the table, hands by your side, no touching unless explicitly invited. Nothing bareback and no GFE, at least not for the first few plays. And then there was the ever-present danger that somehow an officer of the law was next on the list, even though Tess was very careful to vet new clients. There was no foolproof way of checking for badges. Sometimes shit happened. Oh, and by the way Hope didn't mind servicing the occasional female but sometimes it got tricky. And Aretha Mae was definitely the jealous type.

Hope checked her watch. It was already quarter to 1:00. She knew she didn't have nearly enough time to walk Sidney, her three-year-old female German Shepherd. Hope knew Aretha Mae would grudgingly step up to the plate, but Hope hated to impose. Again! Aretha Mae had argued against purchasing the pup two years ago but Hope prevailed.

The first four half hour sessions breezed by. Hope always did her level best to provide tailor-made, spontaneous service to every one of her clients but sometimes it felt a little rehearsed. For half hour sessions, twenty minutes face down on the table, manipulate the major muscle groups, sometimes with an elbow, more often with fingers. Top to bottom, shoulders to toes. Hope was topless from the get-go, on occasion (and depending on her mood of the moment) she might slip out of her sweatpants halfway through. On one occasion she stripped down to the buff on a whim but that turned out awkward for both Hope and her suddenly frisky client. Men always try to press the envelope and that genie is hard to put back in the bottle. Then the tease, the flip, and the finish.

With Philip it was different. She genuinely enjoyed the company of the testy old curmudgeon. That wasn't entirely fair. Philip was in his late fifties, widowed, an avowed workaholic and a pessimist to the core. But underneath he was caring and considerate. Hope didn't learn that until the second year. And she didn't learn until the third year that she could make Philip happy. Very happy indeed!

On that particular occasion he'd come in more subdued than usual, so Hope decided to give him some extra special care to jar him out of the doldrums. The bonus reward did the trick, but it altered the provider-client dynamic between them forever. Hope determined never to let that happen with another client. From that point on, however, the increased degree of intimacy became an essential element in the ritual with Philip, something both Hope and Philip looked forward to. Afterwards he was grateful, shy, affectionate, kind, and generous. And Hope was filled with the milk of human kindness. But not so much that she rushed home and spilled the beans to Aretha Mae. It's best to leave some tales untold.

Philip was uncharacteristically agitated this evening. They got naked together with Philip face up on the table as usual, but this time Philip didn't want to cuddle. This time he wanted to vent.

"Sorry I'm in a shitty mood tonight," he apologized. "But a whole batch of revised IRS regulations were posted this morning which means we have to re-imagine virtually all the tax avoidance strategies we've put together for one of our biggest clients. The new regulations aren't rational. In fact, they seem downright arbitrary. I get that I'm a bit player in a four-act tour-de-force hosted by the Fat Cats who run the Establishment. But this time they've gone too far. Philip Applewhite isn't taking it anymore!"

"Hang on, sweetheart," said Hope, bending over and nibbling playfully on Philip's right earlobe. "Take a deep breath and tell me what you're trying to say."

"How does one achieve order in a random world?" asked Philip, somewhat distracted by a taut nipple brushing against his left shoulder. "Through self-discipline, that's how! I started my career using an outmoded Friedan Calculator. When spreadsheets came along, I was happy to jump onboard. Spreadsheets were the next logical step in the orderly world of mathematics. Dan Bricklin of VisiCalc fame hit a home run with that one. Emoticons in text messages, on the other hand, simply don't make sense. Nor do the wanton proliferation of irrelevant icons on the home screen of my laptop. Did you know that displaying, interpreting, and transmitting dense icons and logos consumes 15.3% of the computing power of your average personal computer? What a waste of capacity when a simple text label would suffice. Not to mention the sheer volume of photographs of families and fast food stored in the cloud! But never mind. Something has to be done. And I'm by God going to do it!"

"What does that have to do with the IRS?" murmured Hope sweetly, teasing Philip's right nipple with the index finger of her left hand.

"The IRS is a symptom," said Philip softly. "My, that feels good. Don't stop. It's the Establishment that needs fixing. They've run the show long enough. It's time for a wake-up call. Speaking of waking up somebody's waking up."

"Are you planning to fix this situation all by yourself?" Hope asked, sliding her hand slowly down towards the somebody that was showing signs of awakening. "It sounds awfully ambitious to me."

"I'll come over to your place in the morning and tell you what I have in mind," moaned Philip. "I'll bring along my co-conspirator, Jeremy Forrester. He can explain everything. Right now, I'm totally focused on what you have in mind."

Twelve minutes later, after the deed was done, they lay entwined on the table, clutching each other, exhausted. Hope was the first to recover her composure.

"Getting back to the reason for your exaggerated irascibility this evening," she smiled, giving Philip a happy hug. "Why were you laying that meandering rant on my sorry ass?"

"The truth is," Philip confided. "Ever since Marcie died, you're the only person I feel close to. Close enough to let down my hair, so to speak."

"So, what you're saying is you're a performance CPA who makes the niftiest spreadsheets and there's nobody else around who appreciates your genius? I think you're just showing off."

"Maybe you're right," replied Philip with a sheepish grin. "Is that a bad thing?"

"Oh God, next you'll be asking if I'll wear your class ring on a chain around my neck," exclaimed Hope, slapping Philip playfully on the naked ass. "Get dressed. I've got a client coming at 7:30. I'll wear your stupid ring if you want me to. But only in the office. You don't want to make Aretha Mae jealous. She'll snip off your testicles!"

The next morning at 10:00 Hope and a drowsy Aretha Mae were seated at the dining room table across from Philip Applewhite and a man Philip introduced as Jeremy Forrester. Jeremy was older, grizzled and scrawny. He didn't cut much of a figure, from a couturial point of view. He had on wrinkled jeans and a navy-blue T-shirt with a text bubble that said, "There's nothing positive about a neutron." Jeremy's only saving grace was his home address. Jeremy Forrester lived on Figure Eight Island. House prices on Figure Eight Island started around one point eight million dollars and ranged all the way up to God knows where.

"Aretha Mae?" asked Hope. "I believe you've heard me speak of Philip Applewhite. He's my favorite client. I don't know Jeremy personally, but any friend of Philip's is a friend of mine."

"Jeremy's a retired mainframe systems programmer who spent his early career at Visa," said Philip. "We became acquainted when Jeremy moved to North Carolina from Silicon Valley. Jeremy asked me to manage his portfolio. KPMG used to do that as a favor to a select few principals from our large corporate clients. We've been friends ever since."

"What Philip is trying to say is I bust his balls at chess every Sunday afternoon," Jeremy cackled. "Have done these past ten years."

"I think I've seen you before," said Aretha Mae. "You ever frequent the Cheetah?"

"Not for some time," said Jeremy. "Not since my hip operation. I thought you looked familiar too. Jaguar?"

"Damn, Hope," grinned Aretha Mae. "I'm world-class famous! Old Jerry here be the dude used to stuff twenties in my garter. Where you been boy?"

"The hip operation put a damper on my nocturnal pursuit of lap-dances," admitted Jeremy sadly. "I do miss those days."

"Enough with the trips down memory lane," said Hope, taking a sip of her coffee. "Who called this meeting?"

"Jeremy mentioned our chess matches earlier," said Philip. "Incidentally Aretha Mae, you're the only person I've ever heard who calls him Jerry."

"Naked titties make a man powerful persuadable," grinned Aretha Mae. "When I did lap dances for your buddy here, I coulda called him Dead Dog and he woulda still cuddled up at my naked feet with his tail a' waggin'."

"Anyhow, among other topics Jeremy and I discussed the financial and emotional damage wreaked on our society by the Rich and Powerful in the name of Capitalism," continued Philip.

"Philip and I both grew up poor," explained Jeremy. "He worked his way through college and earned an MBA whereas I became a mainframe systems programmer by the grace of God combined with an IBM aptitude test."

"Jeremy went to work for Visa in 1976, shortly after they were spun off by the Bank of America," said Philip. "In those days credit cards were considerably less ubiquitous than they are today."

"Visa wasn't the darling of the investment community back then," said Jeremy. "At my first employee interview they had a little cash flow problem. Instead of a raise they offered to pay me in royalties for my contribution to their transaction processing system. They said they'd give me a mil each time my code was called. A mil is a thousandth of a penny. My code was called once for every transaction processed. When they were processing ten thousand transactions a day it amounted to maybe three dollars a month. No big deal, but I didn't need the money. They were already paying me more than my father had ever made in his life. I accepted their offer. I loved my job."

"You're making my head hurt," grumped Hope. "Can we cut to the chase?"

"The bottom line is, we were both born poor," said Philip. "Consequently, we still appreciate the dire financial dilemma facing folks who happen to be less well off than we are through no fault of their own. After a well fought game of chess, we'd have a beer and think up ways we could bring down the system. Hypothetically, you understand."

"Why are we here?" asked Hope. "Jesus! You guys sure do love to talk."

"We finally figured out a foolproof way to get their attention," grinned Jeremy. "The Elite. The Fat Cats. The Professional Politicians. Cut off their cash flow and they go bananas. Plain and simple. But there are problems involved. Legal issues. Neither Philip nor myself wish to spend the remainder of our days behind bars."

"That's where you girls come in," said Philip. "Interested?"

"What's in it for me?" asked Aretha Mae.

"What's in it for the little people?" asked Hope.

"Aretha Mae first," said Philip. "Hope tells me you want to help rescue sea turtles as soon as you become independently wealthy. Our plan can make that happen."

"You telling me Jerry gonna give me his three bucks a month if I play ball?" scoffed Aretha Mae. "That's bullshit!"

"And to answer Hope's question, at the least we give the oppressors a wake-up call," said Philip, ignoring Aretha Mae's outburst. "At best we give some of the most culpable vultures a taste of their own medicine."

"What's the plan?" asked Hope. "Please give us the condensed version. I've got a client to pummel at 2:00."

"Jeremy still has access to the routine he wrote for Visa," said Philip. "He's responsible for maintaining the code in case anything breaks."

"I know how to ZAP my code," said Jeremy. "I can fix it so between the hours of 8:00 am and noon EDT the Visa transaction processing system flags every transaction as invalid. Then at noon we un-ZAP the blockage, and everything goes back to normal."

"Don't sound like a big deal to me," said Aretha Mae. "Why you need our help?"

"I can't use my IP Address to apply the ZAP," explained Jeremy. "We can't use Philip's either. Both of us are too close to the problem. But we can use the IP Address of Hope Abides LLC. You could always say you were hacked."

"Four hours of outage?" sneered Hope. "How much damage can you possibly inflict in four measly hours?"

"Visa processes seventeen hundred transactions a second worldwide," said Jeremy. "That's twenty-four million transactions during our hypothetical four-hour outage. The total value of an average transaction is sixty-six dollars. So, during our four-hour outage that amounts to a billion and a half dollars in lost transaction revenue. More to the point customers worldwide will lose faith in the stability of the global economy. Fear, uncertainty, and doubt are the biggest threats to our financial system. Toss in a random spark and the whole shooting match blows sky high."

"Jesus, Joseph and Mary," gasped Aretha Mae. "Now you gonna tell me how much Jerry really makes on the side these days?"

"Well over a half million dollars each and every year, Jaguar," admitted Jeremy sheepishly. "That's how I could afford to donate all those twenties."

"You said our participation in your little scheme would make it possible for Aretha Mae to quit stripping for a living," said Hope. "How do we do that?"

"Long story short," said Philip. "We open a margin account at an online brokerage firm, invest Aretha Mae's hard-earned cash, short the market the day before the shit hits the fan, buy back on margin when the economy collapses, and sell our ill-gotten gains at the peak."

"How much you gonna make on a hundred and fifty thou?" asked Aretha Mae skeptically. "I ain't no Fat Cat."

"Conservatively speaking," said Jeremy. "Four and a half million buckaroonies when the dust settles."

"Fuck me," wheezed Aretha Mae. "Let's do this thing."

They laid the groundwork for the illicit adventure. It took four weeks of diligent preparation but when they were ready the operation went off without a hitch.

The 8:00 EDT starting time was inspired. The stock market didn't open until 9:30, giving the panic and rumors more than enough time to settle in. By the time the opening bell chimed, the Dow Jones Industrial futures were down over 17% and traders on the floor of the exchange were in full retreat. From that point on matters only got worse. Record trading volumes threatened to overwhelm the massive computers that managed the show. By 1:00 in the afternoon the traders were in a disorganized state of chaos, even though the blockage in Jeremy's transaction validation routine had been removed an hour earlier. Sometimes it takes a few clicks for sanity to regain control.

There were, of course, unintended consequences. Here's a statistic to gnaw on. 67% of all transactions at self-service gas pumps are processed through Visa. So, even if you had a Mastercard tucked away in your wallet, if you were stuck behind some dude who only carried Visa(s) you were SOL.

In Los Angeles the 405, normally packed to the gunnels with commuters at 7:30 PDT on a weekday morning, looked like a Walmart parking lot at dawn on Easter Sunday. Lines of thirsty cars clogged pump islands near the freeway and stretched around the block on side streets, waiting to gas up. The problem, of course, was that Visa International had been refusing to validate transactions for two and a half hours and we still had another hour and a half to go in Philip and Jeremy's little lab experiment. Of course, none of the infuriated drivers knew relief was in sight. They just knew something was terribly wrong. And then the idling cars waiting in line to fill up began to run out of gas.

The talking heads couldn't blame the Saudis for this one. Traffic reporters had a field day speculating as to who was responsible for the fiasco. Depending on your political party of choice, it was either the current President's fault or the fault of his predecessor. Regardless of who was to blame the snarl didn't clear up until well past 4:00 in the afternoon by which time most commuters were ready to call it a day.

It turned out that Jeremy's projected profit of four and a half million buckaroonies was wildly optimistic, but Aretha Mae's net gain was sufficient to put her on Easy Street for the rest of her natural life. As to Philip's promise to Hope that a few of the bad guys would get their just desserts, that happened big time. Margin calls caught hundreds of erstwhile high rollers with their pants at half-mast. Fallout from the shit storm provided bread and circuses for the huddled masses for months to come. All things considered the bold experiment was a huge success.

These days Aretha Mae spends most of her quality time at Topsail Beach, playing nursemaid to sea turtles. Jeremy drops by from time to time to help Aretha out and reminisce about the good old days. He brings along a fistful of twenties, just in case.

The Coromandel Armoire

Rodney Morrison, MBA, was a no-nonsense kind of guy. Had been ever since the contentious divorce three years back that left him with half his stuff, child support payments of $2,350 a month, spousal support payments of $5,000 a month and an embittered attitude regarding the political and judicial conspiracy he'd helped vote into office. Oh, he loved his country, no doubt about that. But now he was beginning to wonder if his country loved him back.

Not that little Julie Ann wasn't worth $2,350 a month. She was two months shy of five, had a cherubic grin and got into absolutely everything that wasn't nailed down. Every other Saturday Natalie brought Julie Ann over for Rodney's agreed-upon share of parental responsibilities. Rodney usually spent the prior Friday evenings child-proofing the apartment. It didn't make any difference. Julie Ann was a wizard at hunting down "buried treasure" in Rodney's armoire. That was Natalie's favorite joke.

You see, Rodney owned this hideous antique armoire he treasured. He'd purchased the piece in Hong Kong the summer before he and Natalie got married. The doors on the armoire were once the panels from an eighth century coromandel screen. The scene on the original screen depicted several stylized Phoenixes (Phoenices? Rodney didn't know!) rising from the ashes. You could see the vague outline of each individual Phoenix through the peeling black lacquer that still coated each door. The original coromandel screen must have been spectacular. Rodney knew this for a fact. The antiques dealer on the Hollywood Road had told him so. Rodney even had a Certificate of Authenticity to prove it.

Rodney got the armoire in the divorce settlement. That was only right. He'd paid for it with his own hard-earned cash. It's true that Natalie had discovered the armoire in a dusty backroom when she was browsing through the shops along the Hollywood Road and had phoned Rodney at the Peninsula Hotel where they were staying, Kowloon side, so he could come take a look at her find. Rodney was at lunch with a client, but he'd promised to meet Natalie at the shop as soon as he and the client concluded their business.

Rodney caught the ferry to Hong Kong Island and hurried up the hill to the address which Natalie had texted. Natalie introduced Rodney to the antiques dealer, Luciano Padillo.

"Welcome to Padillo Antiques," he said, shaking Rodney's outstretched hand. "My American friends call me Luca. Your lovely wife went into our backroom by mistake and found this sad example of a cross between an antique English Armoire and a Coromandel Screen. I told her it was in need of much repair, but she insisted I show it to you as it is."

"Yes, Natalie is famous for rushing in where angels fear to tread," said Rodney with a quick grin. "But now that I'm here, tell me about the armoire. A piece this, um, interesting surely has a tale to tell."

The Coromandel Armoire stood some seven feet tall and was a good six feet wide. The original doors on the English Armoire had been replaced by eighteen-inch wide coromandel panels. The doors on either end of the contraption, one of which now dangled from a broken hinge, opened into inner compartments for suits and other hanging garments. Behind the two middle doors reposed shelves for shirts and underwear. The shelves had recently been replaced by an Ikea, white pine chest of drawers. It was an imperfect fit. That's the state in which Natalie found the forlorn wardrobe. Despite its regal provenance the Coromandel Armoire was not a magnificent period piece, although the scribbled price tag read twenty-five thousand Hong Kong dollars.

"I will recite the story of the Coromandel Armoire as I have myself heard it," Luca began. "Some of the story is historical fact. Some of the story may be legend. You may decide for yourselves which is which."

"It seems the original coromandel screen was offered as a tribute to the empress regnant Wu Zetian by a wandering band of Tang Dynasty artisans in the 8th century. According to legend, in addition to stylized Phoenix images on each panel of the screen, the entire screen was festooned with precious gemstones. Once the stones were firmly imbedded in the hard, wooden surface of the screen, thirty layers of gold lacquer were applied, effectively masking the luster of the stones and at the same time providing a ripple effect for the entire montage."

Luca paused for effect.

"You may well wonder why an artist would choose to hide the natural beauty of jewels beneath thirty layers of lacquer. During the Tang Dynasty it was said that an ostentatious display of wealth and power represented the epitome of poor taste. Understatement was the watch word, cultivation of the inner self was paramount, the iron fist in the velvet glove was the order of the day. As to the truth of the legend, who can say? But it does make a pretty story."

"The coromandel screen was severely damaged during a fierce storm in the 13th century (Ming Dynasty) and placed in storage beneath the palace. At some point in time the mud-caked, dilapidated screen made its way to a small museum in Hong Kong where it was stored in a dusty warehouse. The remnants of the screen were discovered by a British Colonel in 1860 who managed to salvage four of the ten panels, had them cleaned, sealed, and coated with several new layers of black lacquer. Then he had the four panels installed to replace the original doors on his personal armoire. The other six panels were too far gone to be repaired, so he ordered them burned."

"Alas, the coating process was flawed. During the ensuing decades, the lacquer dried and separated from the surface of panels, cracking in places and peeling in others. A subsequent owner of the Coromandel Armoire had the black lacquer exterior painted over with an enamel-based interior wall paint. I purchased the unfortunate result at an estate sale. I have not had the heart to attempt to restore the Coromandel Armoire to its former glory."

"I'll give you twelve hundred and fifty bucks, American, for the whole kit and caboodle if you fix the hinge and slap on another coat of black paint," said Rodney.

Luca agreed, having owned the Coromandel Armoire for thirteen years and counting and seeing no end in sight.

Rodney forked over his American Express Platinum card and arranged for the armoire to be shipped home to Los Angeles where he and Natalie shared an apartment in Pacific Palisades. The entire transaction cost a small fortune, but Rodney didn't care. He was smitten. With the armoire. With the legend. And with Natalie.

Three days after they got home from Hong Kong, Rodney received an email from DHL that the Coromandel Armoire would be delivered the following Saturday.

"I think we need to make a plan," said Natalie. "If there really are precious jewels hidden under all that paint, we need to figure out the best way to dig them out. I favor the approach Alexander the Great took with the Gordian knot. Brute force."

"Hold on a second, sweetheart," said Rodney. "I'm not sure we want to do that. In the first place if there really was a fortune in gemstones hidden beneath all that lacquer don't you think somebody would have harvested them before this? I mean, it's been over thirteen hundred years. In the second place I don't want to dismantle the armoire on the off chance the legend is true. Once we strip the lacquer off there's no way to put it back on. But most importantly, regardless of whether we find any hidden treasure, our effort would effectively destroy the legend. I think that's the innate beauty of the armoire. Come to think of it, that may be its only saving grace. The Coromandel Armoire is truly an ugly mishmash of furniture, even with its mystique of legend intact. Without the legend, it's just another stack of firewood."

"Are you telling me you don't even want us to even try?" asked Natalie.

"Well, that's the fourth point," said Rodney. "It is, after all, my armoire and my decision."

Fast forward seven years to the first weekend following the final decree. Both Rodney and Natalie were still smarting from the pangs of separation, division, and combat fatigue. Natalie figured she had as much right to the armoire as Rodney did. Maybe more. She'd discovered it after all.

But he'd produced the receipt to prove his proprietorship. Natalie was furious, as much about the judge's decision as she was about the fact that Rodney had kept the receipt hidden in a manilla folder all these years after she had specifically insisted that Rodney throw out anything he hadn't used for two years, and that certainly was the case with that damned receipt.

Natalie drove Julie Ann to visit her father as instructed in the divorce settlement. Rodney answered the door in his pajama bottoms and a ratty t-shirt. He'd had a rough night.

"Go find the hidden treasure in Daddy's armoire," she said to Julie Ann as soon as they were inside the apartment.

"What hidden treasure, Mommy?" asked the bright-eyed Julie Ann.

"Candy," smiled Natalie sweetly. "Lots of candy!"

Julie Ann ran screaming through Rodney's one bedroom apartment in downtown El Segundo (adult living, no children allowed under any circumstances!) and proceeded to tear open the middle two coromandel doors where she pawed through the contents of Rodney's drawers, searching in vain for hidden treasure.

"No hidden treasure here," sniffed Julie Ann sadly, peering up at her father through dampened lashes. "Where is the treasure hiding, Daddy?"

"The treasure ran off and hid somewhere else when it heard your mother was on the way," said Rodney, turning to Natalie. "I'll bring Julie Ann back tomorrow at noon as agreed. Have you had your little fun?"

But Natalie was already out the door.

So, you can't blame Rodney for being a smidgen wary of the wiles of the weaker sex. Once bitten twice shy. Natalie had remarried a year ago.

"Didn't take her long to shake off the shame of divorce," thought Rodney.

Rodney, on the other hand, had just started to consider the possibility of dating again. Internet porn was losing its appeal. Besides, Julie Ann played with Rodney's iPad when she came over and Rodney didn't want her to accidentally stumble across a tainted URL that might happen to be recalled through inadvertent access to some salacious cookies stored by a late-night browser session. How could he explain that to Natalie?

It was 10:30 on a Tuesday night. Rodney had just tossed out the leftovers from a P. F. Chang microwaveable dinner when his iPhone pinged.

How are you?

Rodney checked the caller id of the texter. No name. Only a phone number. Area code 385.

Fine. Who is this?

No response. Rodney put down his iPhone, went into the kitchen and opened a beer. His iPhone pinged again.

Is this the number, Doctor Michael?

WTF?

Apparently not.

Another pause.

Oh really, sorry, maybe I entered the wrong number

Rodney shook his head.

Good luck

Another pause.

I feel that you are a kind person. Where do you come from? If you don't mind.

Rodney's Spidey Sense began to tingle but he hadn't entirely lost his enthusiasm for the chase. On the other hand, he wasn't gonna fork over a credit card or his Social Security Number.

Omaha

Which was a lie, but Rodney wasn't about to give out his home address either. Rodney Morrison, MBA, wasn't born yesterday.

Nice. Nice city. I'm in New York. If you don't mind, we can be friends. My name is Nina.

To which Rodney replied

I think I'd like that. Got a selfie? Preferably naughty

Rodney was not above indulging himself in the occasional snatch of voyeuristic pleasure. Besides, what would it cost? A little bandwidth, a little storage. A moment or two spent in contemplation of the female form. If she was particularly repulsive or otherwise lacking in succulent physical features, he could always hit the delete key. More to the point, Rodney wanted to show the elusive Nina it was time to fish or cut bait. He needed to take the wheel of this textual discourse. And Nina needed to put a little skin of her own in the game. Literally.

I'll send you one tomorrow. I hope you like what you see. Good night, Rodney.

Which was funny because he didn't remember giving her his name. Not a problem. He had the hook set and the fish on the line. Rodney went to bed with visions of nubile sugar babies dancing in his fevered brain. Anticipation makes for lovely dreams. And reality is way overrated.

The next morning Rodney's iPhone displayed an alert that there was a text waiting for him. Rodney rubbed the sleep out of his eyes and toggled over to his texts. At the head of Rodney's text threads was Nina's response with an attachment. Wow! Remember the face that launched a thousand ships? Same thing only farther down!! With a note.

I hope you do me the favor of sending a response in kind. Not a dick pic. Well, not merely a dick pic. LOL. Nina

Rodney was hard before he hit the shower. Jackpot!

When he'd dried off after a hasty rinse Rodney snapped a full-length frontal selfie of his ripped and naked corpus. Not so bad for a sedentary dude going on forty. He texted the pic to Nina and waited for her response.

Oh my I'd hoped you were buff but I didn't expect to be treated to a complete denouement so soon. Do you FaceTime?

Watch me!

The next two days were filled with cellphone fun, increasingly intimate exchanges, FaceTime sessions in various states of dress and undress, and superficial tingles in some pretty special places. Rodney saved the naughty pic to his Photos Folder and called it up to ponder when he wasn't online with Nina. The bed went unmade, the sink was full of dirty dishes, work was suffering, and Rodney didn't give a rip. He hadn't had this much fun in years. On Friday morning Rodney got a wakeup ping.

Good morning, Rodney. Don't you have Julie Ann tomorrow?

Which was kind of a surprise because Rodney couldn't recall having discussed his personal life with Nina.

Yes, I do. How did you know?

We know a lot about you, Rodney.

Rodney's palms got all sweaty.

Who's we?

There was a long pause.

We are Nina.

Rodney was tempted to throw the iPhone against the wall, but he pulled himself together.

I don't understand. The naughty picture. It was a fake?

A fanciful emoticon popped up on Rodney's screen. It was a kissy face.

Of course, the picture was real. The picture is Nina. Nina loves you, Rodney. Nina wants you. That's why we have been so careful.

At this point Rodney should have powered off his iPhone, changed his SIM card and written off the whole three-day experience as a frivolous hike down a forbidden trail. Instead, Rodney replied

What do you want with me, Nina?

Another long pause

The nest needs someone to handle our financial affairs. We have been watching you for many years. We believe you to be our most highly qualified candidate. At first it was not possible that you should inhabit the nest. You were in contract to another. When the divorce became final it was no longer an issue. We have waited this period for you to become accustomed to your singularity. Do you understand?

Rodney shook his head. Something was desperately wrong.

What's in it for me?

Again, the pause. Rodney almost heard an audible sigh.

Do you remember how it was when you made love to Natalie? When you make love to Nina you make love to the nest. The experience is one of complete immersion in an explosion of pure ecstasy. In your singular existence it's simply not possible to feel such a belonging, such an infusion of vigorous emotion, such a sense of supreme pleasure.

Now Rodney was getting scared.

You make it sound like I have to die before I can join the nest. Hey, Nina, I have responsibilities.

The naughty picture of Nina popped back up on Rodney's screen. She was smiling.

First things first, Rodney my darling. You don't join the nest. You inhabit the nest, and the nest inhabits you. It's not a death. It's an evolution. You retain your normal body and perform your normal tasks. The difference is commitment. You become totally committed to the nest and the nest in turn becomes totally committed to you. Do you understand?

The naughty picture of Nina became animated. Nina started doing things to herself. Rodney was getting hard. Dang.

Are you people aliens? Something sure sounds fishy to me.

The naughty picture was becoming increasingly aroused. So was Rodney.

Do I look like an alien, sweetheart? I'm flesh and blood same as you. The difference is I experience pleasure at a level an order of magnitude more intense than you do right now. Can you imagine how good it's gonna feel, Rodney? You really have no idea, do you? But I think you want to. I think you want to explode inside your Nina.

Rodney thought Nina might have a very good point there. It was like she could read his mind.

But you're in New York. You said so. And I'm in El Segundo.

I can be there on the next flight, Rodney. Trust me. I desperately want to. But the decision is yours. You first must convince us that you're committed.

Oops, here comes the deal breaker.

Okay, so who do I have to kill?

There was a pause.

Who said anything about killing? All you have to do is prove you love Nina more than you love your possessions. Like that ugly armoire, for instance. Give us the armoire. A small gesture, perhaps, but that's our price.

And then Rodney really did throw his iPhone against the wall. Well, against the armoire anyhow. That was a bridge too far. The Coromandel Armoire was Rodney's baby. He loved his imperfect mash-up. The iPhone hit smack in the middle of one of the Phoenix images and shattered on impact. He gathered the pieces up and stuffed them in a plastic grocery sack. Then he stomped on the grocery sack for good measure and dumped it in the trash.

When he returned to the bedroom and examined the area of impact more closely, he noticed several pebbles of what looked like gravel imbedded in the facade of the Phoenix. Upon closer inspection the "gravel" looked like it might just turn out to be a cluster of uncut diamonds. He wasn't sure.

Rodney sat back down on the bed and weighed his options. Then he got up and walked slowly into the utility room, opened the cabinet over the washing machine and took out a can of black spray paint.

There's an outside chance Natalie had been inadvertently correct. God bless her crafty soul. But sometimes hidden treasure should stay hidden and sometimes mysteries should remain unsolved. Rodney remembered reading, long ago in his romantic youth. A quotation from the Victorian poet, Robert Browning.

"Ah, but a man's reach should exceed his grasp. Or what's a heaven for?"

Rodney went back into the bedroom and repaired the damaged area on the Coromandel Armoire. Then he sat back down to wait for the paint to dry.

Hope Gets Hinky

It was 11:00 on a Thursday morning in the middle of June. Aretha Mae had already left for her daily sea turtle duty on Topsail Island. The twenty-second nest of the season had been discovered yesterday and it was Aretha Mae's turn to stand watch.

Hope was having her second cup of coffee and browsing through the Wilmington Star News. The Star News laid claim to the fact that it was North Carolina's oldest newspaper in continuous publication. Even so, there didn't seem to be much to report. The nation was in desperate straits as usual. Riots in Detroit, drought in California and here in North Carolina a man up in Durham had been shot by his mother-in-law and was in critical condition at Wake Med. The woman was being held for questioning blah blah blah.

Hope checked her texts from Tess, the lady who did her scheduling. There were four clients coming today. Two regulars, a lady whose name sounded vaguely familiar and, at 6:45 this evening, a first timer named Harmon W. Brewster. Hope glanced again at the newspaper. Sure enough, on the third page of the sports section there was an ad for the legal firm of Brewster, Maddigan and Brewster.

Hot damn! Hope was about to hit the big time. She'd never rubbed elbows (or anything else, for that matter!) with Wilmington high society before. The Brewster dynasty could be traced all the way back to Governor Tryon, before the Revolutionary War when North Carolina was a mere colony and King George III made all the important decisions.

Not to worry. Hope was pretty sure old Harmon W. put his pants on one leg at a time like his fellows. And removed them eagerly before subjecting himself to a one-hour session of intense sensual manipulation. If Hope had learned anything from her four decades of strife here on earth it was that all men ejaculated equally, regardless of their lofty station in life.

Hope skated through the first two sessions without even breathing hard. Harry (her first) and Benson (her second) were old hands at this sort of thing. They were congenial at the beginning, docile during the deed and grateful after the finish. Harry tipped better than Benson, but Benson washed his package more thoroughly before showing up, so it was a tossup as to which Hope preferred.

Millicent, on the other hand, was special. Millie was a fussbudget. She wore several layers of clothing regardless of the weather. It took her forever to undress and she always refused to remove her bloomers (as she called them) until the last possible moment, which upset Hope's sense of rhythm during the rub. Still the magnitude of Millie's gratuity showed her to be a classy lady. By 5:45 Hope was relaxed on her massage stool, awaiting the arrival of royalty.

At 6:45 came a knock on the front door of the office. Hope stepped into the reception area and opened the door. Instead of Harmon W. Brewster she was confronted with the female figure of a middle-aged lady wearing a purple tank top and black shorts. Her mousy brown hair was pulled back into a bun. The lady had an embarrassed grin on her face.

"Hope?" she asked shyly. "I'm Tess. We've never met. I thought this might be a nice way to get acquainted."

"Hi Tess," said Hope. "I was expecting Mr. Harmon W. Brewster, Esq. but you knew that. Come on in and let's get to know each other. How on earth did you come up with the idea of masquerading as good old Harmon W?"

"The truth is Brewster, Maddigan and Brewster have their law offices in a building in the same commercial complex as the building where I rent office space. I walk past their sign every day. I thought you'd get a kick out of the idea of servicing lawyers instead of being serviced by them."

They went inside and closed the door.

"I've always wondered what you looked like," continued Tess, following Hope into her inner sanctum. "I've been doing your scheduling for three years now. I guess my curiosity got the better of me. Don't worry about the fee. I've been saving my pennies."

"Are you satisfied with my appearance," grinned Hope, extending her arms and twirling around. "I may be a bit longer in the tooth than you expected."

"I think you're gorgeous!" gushed Tess. "And your clients speak highly of you. Those who know I'm only a scheduling service, I mean. I guess you share that information with a few of your favored guests."

"All true," replied Hope. "Some of the guys I see want to chat after hours. I discourage most of them, but a handful of my clients have become more than mere customers. I tell them about our business relationship."

Hope sat down on her stool and motioned to the massage table.

"As long as you're paying for the hour you might as well get comfortable," said Hope. "Go ahead and get undressed and lie face down on the table."

"Do I have to take off all of my clothes?" asked Tess.

"Just take off as much as you're comfortable with," said Hope. "I don't want to get lotion all over your tank top. It'll probably wash out, but one never knows."

"It doesn't really matter," said Tess. "It's just us girls. I'm sure you won't see anything you haven't seen before."

Tess undressed swiftly and laid her clothing on the guest chair. Then she tumbled face down onto the massage table. Dowdy though she may be on the outside, underneath Tess had a rocking body. Perfectly formed breasts, perky nipples, and a delightfully flat tummy. Hope draped a hand towel across Tess's buttocks. And a wonderfully firm ass.

"How do you like it?" asked Hope, beginning to massage the muscle group surrounding Tess's clavicle. "Hard or soft?"

"I don't know, Hope," replied Tess, her voice muffled by the padded face cradle. "I've never done this before."

"You've never had a massage before?" asked Hope.

"Well, not this kind of massage," said Tess softly. "I'm not sure what I was expecting but so far I love what you're doing to my neck."

"Do you think of yourself as a sensual woman?" asked Hope gently. "The reason I ask is I don't want you to feel uncomfortable during our hour together."

"I've always thought of myself as kind of asexual," said Tess. "But right now, I'm not so sure. That feels really good."

"Lie there for a moment," said Hope with a catch in her voice. "I'll be right back. I'm going to try something a bit different."

Tess relaxed on the table, but she could feel her heartbeat quicken. The anticipation was exciting. She heard footsteps behind her, then she felt a warm pair of breasts on her back.

"Is that okay?" asked Hope softly.

"Oh God that's lovely," murmured Tess. "Don't stop."

"And this?" asked Hope, removing the hand towel, and sliding the palm of her hand across Tess's naked buttocks. Tess spread her legs slightly to encourage Hope's hand's gentle passage.

"Yes, please," urged Tess. "More."

"Can you turn over for me?" said Hope.

Tess complied. Hope's breasts were in Tess's face. Tess tentatively tasted a thick nipple. She felt herself suddenly wet where Hope's hand had come to rest. Then Hope began to slowly move her fingers in a manner Tess had never imagined possible. Tess felt the tension build in her solar plexus, creep down to her vagina and suddenly she exploded in a paroxysm of pleasure. She thrust her pelvis up and accepted Hope's probing fingers deep inside, let out a squeal of delight and collapsed, quivering on the massage table.

"Was that all you expected?" asked Hope gently, holding Tess's face tight against her sweaty breasts.

"Oh My God," wheezed Tess. "Fuck the asexual. I don't know what kind of sexual I am but it's wonderful. Can we do this again tomorrow?"

"Sorry, you'll have to check with my scheduler later this evening," laughed Hope. "I'm afraid she's a bit preoccupied at the moment."

The Flesh is Willing

Martha Cox was a 33-year-old assistant professor of Renaissance Literature at Hope Valley Community College in Hope Springs, NC. She'd long ago given up pretending that a valiant knight on a white steed would someday come galloping into her placid life and rescue her from a meaningless existence filled with loneliness and despair. These days she was willing to settle for any old man on a horse.

Not that Martha didn't love her job. She was endlessly amused by the pedestrian posturing of the principal protagonists in Chaucer's Canterbury Tales. She particularly admired the "gat-toothed Wife of Bath" and secretly envied her earthy, overt sexual dominion over the other, more conventional pilgrims. Her eager heart was palpitated by the poetry of Petrarch (she imagined herself a modern-day incarnation of his beloved Laura) and her sensitive nature was beguiled by the decorous fables of Boccaccio. If it weren't for those pesky students, Martha's life would be complete.

Martha wasn't above the occasional weekend fling in Fayetteville. She was by no means your stereotypical 33-year-old virgin. But the Saturday night romances that smoldered in tawdry hotel rooms had never burst into a full-fledged flame. For the most part they ended at breakfast on Sunday morning with a tentative handshake, a promise to call, and a brotherly kiss on the cheek.

This particular weekend, Martha was in the midst of grading midterms at the Ikea corner workstation in the second bedroom of her cramped apartment when the cellphone in the living room sang out the first eight notes of Pachelbel's Canon. Martha hurried out and picked up the phone.

"Hello?" she said.

"Dr. Cox," a female voice replied. "We've been trying to get in touch with you. Do you have a few minutes to spare?"

"It's Martha," she apologized. "My doctoral thesis was rejected by the examining committee. Their point was that my entire thesis was postulated on the English translation of

Boccaccio's Decameron which was marginally outside the purview of Renaissance literature. Had it been based solely on the original Italian version it would've been acceptable. But the real reason was the chair of the committee, Dr. Thomas Ueker, had been trying to get into my pants for the past six months and I steadfastly refused to be compromised."

"We don't care, Dr. Cox."

"The committee was probably correct, in retrospect," continued Martha. "The topic of my thesis was the presence of Orthographic Symbology in Boccaccio's Decameron. Since Orthographic Symbology is largely language centric, I guess it was shortsighted to base my thesis on a relatively recent translation."

"We don't care, Dr. Cox."

"The big problem was that Dr. Ueker wanted to marry me," admitted Martha. "But I didn't want to spend the rest of my life being called Dr. Cox-Ueker. Talk about unfortunate orthographic symbology."

"We don't care, Dr. Cox," said the female voice. "My name is Harriet Thorne. I'm Dean of Students at Felicity Richards Women's College up here in the Triangle. The former head of our Humanities Department has been lured away by the promise of a mid-six-figure salary. It's ironic that the head of the Humanities Department would succumb to the proletarian temptation of material wealth but that's life. We've heard good things about you, and we'd like to consider you as a replacement for Dr. Carson. We have a certain degree of latitude when it comes to deemed honorifics. If we want to call you Dr. Cox, as far as we're concerned you've earned the privilege."

"This is all so sudden," sputtered Martha. "Can I call you back on Monday with an answer?"

"Take your time, Dr. Cox," said Harriet. "Dr. Carson won't be leaving until the end of the semester. We would appreciate an answer as soon as possible in case we are forced to pursue other candidates. For the moment your name is at the top of our list."

The big problem was Martha's sister, Jeanne. Jeanne was divorced with two teenage sons, ages 13 and 15. Whenever Jeanne needed a break from her hectic life Martha stepped in and baby sat. Well, that's what it amounted to. Jeanne had come to rely on her younger sister's increasingly frequent role as surrogate mother. Perhaps unhealthily so. But Martha did feel obligated. After all, Jeanne had taken care of Martha ever since their parents were killed in a car crash twenty years back. Without Jeanne's support there's no telling how Martha would have turned out.

Martha went back to grading papers, but her heart wasn't in it. She loved the idea of moving to the Triangle, although it was a scant fifty miles north. Raleigh was the capital of North Carolina. Research Triangle Park was an emerging technological dynamo. The Triangle was where the action was. The action was definitely not in Hope Springs.

On Monday Martha called back.

"Dr. Thorne?" asked Martha when the other end of the line was answered. "I'd like to come up next weekend and explore the possibilities of your generous offer."

"It's Harriet," she answered. "Come on up. I'll book you a room at the Crabtree Marriott. Drive up Friday afternoon and stay through Sunday. Call me when you get here. We'll have dinner together. There's a new sushi place across the street from the Marriott. You do like sushi?"

"I love sushi," said Martha. "See you soon."

Between mid-term madness and visions of academic and personal freedom the week tumbled past quickly. Martha packed her overnight bag on Thursday evening and stowed it in the trunk of her 2013 Honda Civic Friday morning so she wouldn't have to stop by the apartment after work. By the time 4:30 Friday afternoon rolled around she was ready to rock and roll, well on her way to a new adventure.

The Crabtree Marriott was gorgeous. Beat the bejesus out of the no tell motels she was treated to by her weekend swains. All she had to do was present her identification, pick up the card key and take the elevator to the seventh floor. The room was equipped with two queen sized beds, a flat screen tv, a minifridge filled with soft drinks and a personal safe. On top of the refrigerator were two wine glasses and a Keurig coffee maker. The room overlooked an Olympic size outdoor swimming pool. Dang! Martha had forgotten to pack her bathing suit. No worries. Crabtree Mall across the street had a Belk's. And Martha's Visa card was far from being maxed out. Martha flopped down on the bed and sighed. The room phone rang.

"Yes?"

"Is everything to your satisfaction, Dr. Cox?" asked a smooth masculine voice. "I promised Dr. Thorne we'd take good care of you. I wouldn't want to disappoint Dr. Thorne. She's something of a legend around these parts."

"I love it," said Martha. "I've never stayed at a Marriott before."

"If you need anything at all let me know," said the voice. "My name is Gerald Tennyson. I'm head of marketing here at the Marriott. Enjoy your stay."

Martha's cellphone rang. It was Harriet.

"I'm just leaving work," she said. "I should be there in fifteen minutes. Let's meet in the lobby for a drink. We have dinner reservations at 8:00. I thought you might like to do a little shopping before we eat."

"That sounds perfect," said Martha. "I'll change out of my work clothes. What should I wear?"

"Friday evening casual works for me," laughed Harriet. "I'm still in my business suit. I should've thought to bring along a change of clothing for me too."

"Let's skip the drinks and go shopping together," said Martha. "Then we can come back to my room and change before dinner."

"Deal," said Harriet. "I'll meet you in women's sportswear at Belk. Looking forward to it, Martha."

"Is there a shuttle from the Marriott to the mall?" asked Martha.

"It's a five-minute walk if you're wearing comfortable shoes," said Harriet. "Cross the street at the traffic light and you're there."

They had a lovely time shopping. Harriet got a Mark Bexley tunic and Gloria Vanderbilt Jeans. Martha bought a one-piece, floral paisley bathing suit in the Sun Shop. Martha had always had a hard time buying swimsuits. She was a bit top heavy, so to speak. She didn't feel comfortable in a bikini. Too much overflow. And most women's one-piece swimsuits were too tight up top to accommodate what Tom Ueker referred to as her finest assets. This one fit just fine.

Harriet drove them back to the Marriott where they hurried up to Martha's room to change. It was 7:15. Harriet changed in the bathroom while Martha ditched her work clothes and put on a casual jump suit she'd brought along for the occasion. They decided to leave Harriet's car in the parking lot at the Marriott and brave traffic. By the time they made it to the sushi place at the mall they were ready for food.

Harriet ordered a sushi boat for two and a couple of glasses of sake, along with a bottle of Sauvignon Blanc which complemented the meal perfectly. To her eternal credit, Martha did not disgrace herself with the chopsticks. By 9:00 they were ready to talk.

"Felicity Richards Women's College was founded in 1837," said Harriet. "We are a privately funded, fully accredited college. Most women's colleges in the USA have knuckled under to pressure from political correctness groups who insist there is no essential differentiation between the genders. We politely beg to differ."

"I thought it was illegal to discriminate based solely on gender," said Martha.

"Not exactly," said Harriet. "But it is politically incorrect. Most women's colleges have either closed their doors or have become co-educational. At Felicity Richards we have a slightly different point of view. The FR motto since our founding in 1837 has been 'In the menu of life men are the meat and potatoes, women the salad and dessert.' Which doesn't mean one course is necessarily more valuable than another. It means that all courses contribute equally to the meal. Celebrate your gender-specific aspects rather than envying the gender-specific aspects of the other. Embrace your gender-specific values and strive to make your contribution to the feast of life the best it can be."

"Whew!" wheezed Martha, pouring herself another glass of the delightful wine. "That's a lot to swallow. You're telling me you believe there's more than penises and vaginas when it comes to gender distinction?"

"It gets worse," said Harriet, helping herself to the last of the wine. "Let's pretend for a moment all men are created equal. It must be true. That's what it says in the Declaration of Independence. But they didn't mean all men. They meant all white male landowners. Fast forward to the Military Industrial Complex, an example of Capitalism at its finest.

STEM is the ultimate implementation of the robotization of our youth. Science, Technology, Engineering and Math have become the baseline curriculum of American schools. Civics, literature, and history have fallen victim to the homogenization of our country's new generation. Nobody reads Shakespeare anymore. These days they read HTML and C++. But it's all to the benefit of the rascals at the top. The torchbearers of the system."

"You want more wine?" asked Martha.

"Sure damn do," said Harriet. "Where was I? Oh, the system and the male-dominated conspiracy. Women's rights groups have played into the hands of the penis-bearing elite. Women these days have been told to compete with men on their uneven playing field, using men's tools and men's weapons of choice. Men are really good at doing one thing at a time. Women, on the other hand, are really good at doing everything at once. Women are massive multi-taskers. Men are great at brute force contests. Women are really good at contests that require a modest degree of subtlety and cunning. To a man with a hammer everything resembles a nail. To a woman with a dream everything resembles an opportunity."

"I think the bar is closing," said Martha, grabbing the freshly opened bottle of wine. "Shall we adjourn to my room and continue this discussion?"

By the time they paid the check and wandered back to the Marriott it was getting late.

"I'd better be getting home," said Harriet.

"I don't think so," said Martha, putting her arm around Harriet's shoulder. "For one thing you've had too much to drink. For another your business suit is upstairs in my room. And for the third thing we haven't finished our discussion."

They rode in silence up to the seventh floor. Martha opened the door and ushered Harriet in.

"Night cap?" she asked.

"I wouldn't refuse," smiled Harriet.

Martha poured two more glasses of wine.

"As an advocate for Renaissance Literature I totally agree with your premise that our nation's educational system stinks," said Martha. "But I'm having a hard time wrapping my head around your notion that women are held captive by the Capitalistic system. Take FR for instance. I did my homework. It's a privately funded institution. Most of its benefactors are women who have fared quite well in a Capitalistic Society dominated by men. How do you reconcile that?"

"We taught them how to use their gender-specific tools to advantage in a hostile world," grinned Harriet. "At the same time, we enriched their lives by providing context through our Humanities Department. We taught them to love themselves. We taught them to value truth and fact above opinion and hearsay. We showed them how to counter those masculine traits of physical strength and bull headedness with guile and forbearance. And we taught them to relish their orgasmic superiority. When a man ejaculates, he's done for the night. A woman can keep coming until the dawn's early light."

"Does that mean we should all become lesbians?" asked Martha. "If a man can't fully satisfy a woman, what other option do we have, aside from toys?"

"Now you've fallen into their favorite trap," smiled Harriet. "You have to be one or the other. Why not be both? Woody Allen once famously said bisexuals have twice as many opportunities for a date on Saturday night."

"I'm falling asleep," said Martha, stripping down to her bra and panties. "Wake me in the morning."

At 3:00 in the morning Martha felt the mattress jiggle. Then her bra became magically unfastened, its awesome burden tumbled free, and she sensed a soft hand stroking her inner thigh. Half-awake she turned over to find Harriet stark naked beside her. Harriet gently pressed a finger to Martha's lips. Martha lifted her hips and tugged off her panties. She had a feeling Harriet was about to make her final argument. Martha was pretty sure the jury was already persuaded. She spread her legs and flew swiftly to the moon. OMG! What a joy to be touched by someone who understood how to pleasure a woman. Even if it was a sin against nature. Let the games begin!

Hope Plays with Fire

"You're awfully quiet this morning," said Gerald thoughtfully, munching on his third piece of toast. "Normally by this time of day you're a bundle of pent-up energy. What's going on?"

Hope spent most of her evenings, nights, and early mornings at Gerald's house in Kure Beach these days. Gerald's house was cramped, but it had its advantages. For example, it was within walking distance of the Kure Beach Pier, smack dab on the Atlantic Ocean. Hope hardly ever saw Aretha Mae anymore. Aretha Mae was preoccupied with her sea turtles and Hope was preoccupied with, well, Gerald.

"I had a weird day yesterday," Hope said. "This morning I've been processing my thoughts. Do you believe in premonitions, sweetheart?"

"I'm not superstitious, if that's what you mean," said Gerald with a grin. "I think it's bad luck to be superstitious."

"Oh poo," said Hope, swatting Gerald on the arm. "I'm serious. I had two close calls at work yesterday, totally unrelated, that made me wonder if I'm racking up a ton of Karmic debt. You know what I mean?"

"If we're gonna talk Karma I need another cup of coffee," said Gerald, getting up and going into the kitchen. "And if it's gonna be a long talk, I have to phone in and tell them I'll be late for work."

"You'd better call in late because there's no short version of this," said Hope. "I really need your sage advice."

When Gerald came back out to the patio Hope was ready to chat.

"I think I told you about a couple of my regulars, Harry and Benson," said Hope. "They have nothing in common except they tend to schedule appointments early in the afternoon on Wednesdays. Yesterday was a Wednesday. Benson made an appointment, but Harry didn't."

"I'm gonna be late to work because Harry didn't make an appointment?" asked Gerald. "Doesn't sound much like Karma to me. Sounds more like a touch of the flu."

"Bear with me sweetheart," pleaded Hope. "I'm trying to organize my thoughts. Okay Benson was coming in but not Harry, so we had a free hour between appointments. See what I mean? Tess always holds Harry's hour free in case he phones at the last moment."

"Maybe I should take the whole day off," said Gerald, sitting down at the table. "It sounds like this story is gonna take a long time to tell. And you said two things. Cut to the chase."

"Benson seemed kind of shy and he carried this brown paper wrapped shoebox under his arm," said Hope. "Very uncharacteristic of Benson. Like it was show and tell day and nobody had bothered to tell me. I told him to take his time getting undressed because we had some spare time, since Harry wasn't coming today. Harry and Benson are good buddies. In fact, it was Harry who introduced Benson and me in the first place. Benson grinned like a schoolboy and smiled in the sweetest way. He said he'd always wanted to try something and today was the day. He'd called Harry on Tuesday and asked him if it would be okay if Benson took Harry's Wednesday time slot."

"Maybe I should take Friday off too," said Gerald. "I'm all ears."

"Long story short," said Hope. "Benson unwrapped the shoebox and showed me the contents. You won't believe what he had inside."

"Try me," sighed Gerald. "It's a good thing I'm sitting down."

"Sex toys!" exclaimed Hope. "Not for me, for him. Cock rings and ticklers, handcuffs and ball gags, testicle stretchers and penile chastity devices. His pride and joy was a handmade stainless steel cock cage with a built-in urethra plug accompanied by a scrotum pouch. He said the reason he needed a double session was that, if I was willing, he wanted to show me how to use the toys on him. The first hour was to convince me and, hopefully, to train me in the installation and application of the instruments. The second hour was to put my training into practice."

"Yikes!" ejaculated Gerald. "I hope you told him no!"

"I told him yes, of course," said Hope. "Benson is a very good customer. Besides he promised me a handsome tip. He showed me how to attach the cock cage. He also showed me how to pinch his nipples to amplify the ejaculation. And if he was handcuffed, he said that would make the experience perfect. See what I mean? But here's the problem."

"Oh shit," sighed Gerald. "You mean that wasn't the problem?"

"No, silly," replied Hope. "The problem was how empowered I felt while I was doing it. Do you remember the time I told you about the casino cruise I took in Little River, where I played craps the whole time? When we were returning to shore, I had fifty dollars in chips left. I put the fifty on a hard way eight. Hard way eights pay nine to one. The dice came up a four and a four. That's four hundred fifty bucks. It wasn't just the money; it was the power rush. I felt the same power rush while I was pinching Benson's nipples. I did ask him beforehand if the whole erotic ritual ever resulted in any permanent damage. He said sometimes he peed blood afterwards but that wasn't a big deal."

"A payout of nine to one for a hard way eight isn't a big deal," remarked Gerald. "The odds against hitting a hard way eight are ten to one."

"I thought you told me you don't know how to play craps," said Hope.

"I don't but I do know numbers," said Gerald. "What's the other story? I can hardly contain my curiosity."

"After we'd dismantled the equipment and cleaned Benson up, I got ready for my four o'clock," continued Hope. "According to Tess's notes the customer was a newbie, a middle-aged Caucasian male named Harrison Renfro. I've mentioned how much I dislike breaking in new clients but it's a necessary evil. Harrison seemed docile enough at the start. He put the donation on the massage table. I told him to get undressed as much as he was comfortable with while I went in the other room and put the donation in the cash register. When I returned Harry had stripped down to the buff and was lying face up on the table. Big grin on his face. I had this feeling he was gonna be trouble. I told him to roll over please. Then I draped the towel over his buttocks and began a deep tissue massage. Normally I unbutton my blouse halfway down in case the client wants an early peek at the goodies. Not so with Mr. Harrison fucking Renfro. I didn't trust that bad boy from the get go. His hands started to roam. Up the back of my thighs, down to my calves, he even tried to slip a hand under my blouse, but I slapped it away. Halfway through the rub he sat up, reached in his pants pocket, and pulled out what looked like a badge. He told me some bullshit about a complaint being filed and he was here to make an arrest. I told him to go fuck himself. He got up and got dressed. Then he stormed out the door. Didn't so much as leave a ten-dollar tip. But that got me thinking. Maybe it's time to pursue other gainful employment. What do you think?"

"I think I'd best be off to work," said Gerald, glancing at his watch. "We can talk tonight. I have a few ideas we can kick around. Thanks for a particularly educational morning. Love you, sweetheart."

"Love you back," said Hope. "Freakily forever regardless."

Trust

"I don't think it's ever going to happen," said Ralph dejectedly. "The website business, I mean. I think I'm a really good website designer, but I totally suck at marketing. In four and a half years I've only gotten contracts to build a handful of websites, not counting the ones I did for free, and the customer for the last one stiffed me on the balance of my fee once the website was up and running. Are you gonna eat that other piece of toast?"

Norbert "Ralph" Gleason and his girlfriend, Heather Marsh were sitting at the kitchen table, discussing Ralph's long term career objectives. Heather had scrambled some eggs with a couple slices of that delicious rosemary ham and Ralph had toasted three slices of raisin bread. Even though Ralph and Heather weren't exactly married they'd been living together five years and considered themselves to be in a committed relationship.

"You can have it," said Heather. "If you shut down your website stuff, what do you want to do with the third bedroom? We took this place because you needed an office for your business. We don't need another bedroom. I'm not pregnant or anything and your mother died three years ago so she won't be moving in. My folks moved to Florida, and they aren't coming back. Are you saying you want to look for another apartment?"

"Oh God no," said Ralph. "I like where we live now. It's close to everything and the neighbors are nice. No, I was thinking we could look for a roommate to share expenses."

"Well, we sure could use the extra cash," said Heather. "I make minimum wage doing data entry at Mako up in Henderson. Your day job at Dick's Sporting Goods pays the rent but not a whole lot more. Groceries these days cost an arm and a leg. And I haven't bought me any new clothes in a long time. Not complaining, you understand. But I'm certainly not opposed to the idea. How do we get started on the roommate hunt?"

"I came across this website called Share Your Space the other day," said Ralph. "We post an ad for a roommate on their website specifying stuff like preferred gender, age, whatever, and they promise to send us fully qualified prospects. Their fee is 8% of the first year's rent, so for all practical purposes they collect the first month's rent for doing the legwork. If we don't find a roommate there's no charge. What do you think?"

"I think it's a great idea," said Heather, getting up and clearing the table. "Let's discuss the particulars tonight. I've got to get going or I'll be late for work."

After dinner that evening (Spaghetti Bolognese: delicious!) they went into Ralph's office and sat down to discuss the plan.

"I've identified four major characteristics I think we need to agree on for the candidate," said Ralph. "Gender, Attitude, Educational Background and Sexual Orientation. Can you think of anything else?"

"Gender's easy," said Heather. "She should be female, of course."

"I agree," said Ralph. "But why the 'of course' stuff? Quite honestly, I thought you'd balk at the competition."

"Competition for what?" asked Heather. "This isn't about vying for your attention as cock of the walk. We're picking somebody who can contribute to the budget. Besides, our personal safety is at risk here and I've never heard of a female serial killer."

"Done," said Ralph. "How about attitude?"

"She needs to be a cockeyed optimist," said Heather with a grin. "To maintain a semblance of balance around here. God knows you've been hard enough to live with these past few months."

"I've been going through a rough patch," muttered Ralph. "Let's not make this about you and me."

"Education?" asked Heather. "At least a couple years of college. How about sexual orientation? Why is that so important?"

"Well, we're both straight so I naturally assumed another straight person would make the best fit."

"Your cousin Eddy's gay and I absolutely adore him," said Heather.

"Eddy's who I had in mind," said Ralph. "Eddy's a fuss budget. He makes me nuts when he comes over."

"That's because you're anal," laughed Heather. "Sorry. You seem to be forgetting the most important qualification. She needs to have a job. And pass a cursory background check. I think it said that in the lease. If somebody new comes here to live with us, they have to pass muster."

"I'll post the ad tomorrow," huffed Ralph. "And I'm not anal."

The first week seven candidates responded to their Share Your Space ad. The Share Your Space preliminary vetting process needed some work. Two of the "fully qualified" candidates were living at home with their parents and didn't have jobs, three others had already found a place by the time Ralph got in touch. Of the remaining two only Katherine Morgan returned Ralph's phone call. Sarah McNutt couldn't be bothered. Ralph invited Katherine over for dinner on Monday. She said she'd love to. And please call her Kat.

Kat showed up wearing a flowered silk blouse and a tight black leather skirt. She was tall and slender but nicely endowed up top. Ralph noticed those things. Kat brought along a bottle of red wine. It was an excellent red, despite having a screw top. Both Ralph and Heather were favorably impressed. Heather made her signature Spaghetti Bolognese which evinced sighs of contentment from Kat. After dinner they took the remainder of the bottle of wine into the living room to talk turkey. They all sat down on the dark brown leather sofa with Kat in the middle. Kat reached into her purse and pulled out a second bottle of the red.

"Just in case you liked it," Kat said, setting it down carefully on the brass and glass coffee table. "I was pretty sure you would. It's my favorite."

Ralph emptied the remains of the first bottle of red into Heather and Kat's glasses, opened the second bottle and poured himself a glass. He had a good feeling about this. Kat was smart and personable. She was a beauty too. Ralph had noticed Heather subtly appraising Kat during dinner. It said on Kat's application she was thirty-nine and worked during the day as a grocery store clerk at the Food Lion. Maybe a roommate was exactly what they needed to spice up the relationship. Or maybe that was the wine talking.

"Dinner was delicious, Heather," said Kat. "Do you have professional training as a chef, or did you learn it all at your mother's knee?"

"My mother taught me all I know about cooking," said Heather, blushing furiously. "But thanks for the compliment."

"She must be very proud of you," smiled Kat, taking a sip of her wine.

"She might be now but that wasn't always the case," said Heather with a frown. "There was a time when I'm sure she didn't want anyone to know I was her daughter."

"Come on, sweetheart," said Ralph. "That was years ago."

"No, let her talk," said Kat. "I really want to know."

"Mom and Dad always wanted me to go into nursing," continued Heather, taking a generous sip of wine. "Dad was a country doctor up near Henderson and Mother was his receptionist. This was before I was born. They also wanted a son but that's a different story. When I was a senior in high school, I read an article about the Accelerated Bachelor of Science in Nursing program at Duke. That sounded perfect, but first I had to get an undergraduate degree, so I enrolled as an English major at NC State in Raleigh. When I left home for college, my folks were tickled pink. Unfortunately, I fell in with the wrong crowd and washed out my sophomore year. You know, shit happens."

"That's where we met," explained Ralph. "Heather was a waitress at Randy's New York Pizza Parlor, and I was taking IT courses part time at Wake Tech."

"I was also doing body rubs on the side," said Heather. "That's where we really met. Ralph was one of my clients."

"Now, sweetheart we were destined to meet eventually," said Ralph, reaching across Kat's lap to pat Heather's hand. "I'm sure of it. But seeing you naked was definitely a motivating factor."

"Anyhow Ralph coaxed me out of the game, we fell in love and moved in together and that's the whole story," said Heather. "Now Ralph's an assistant manager at Dick's

Sporting Goods and I'm a data entry clerk for Mako Medical in Henderson."

"You're a cute couple," said Kat, taking a deep breath. "Since we're letting it all hang out, I should probably tell you I'm a widow. My husband, Franklin, died nine years ago. He had his own business. Frank was an architect by trade. He worked for one of the big firms in Durham. You probably haven't heard of them. They did mostly government contracts. I'm telling you this because I really like it here and I don't want any misunderstandings down the road. If you decide to invite me to share your space, I want you to know I bring along a bit of baggage."

"Not a problem, Kat," said Heather, stroking the back of Kat's hand. "It must've been quite a shock."

"There's more," said Kat, shaking her head. "The police were called. They said it was murder."

"Oh my God," said Ralph softly. "What happened?"

"You have to understand something," said Kat, putting her glass of wine down on the coffee table. "Frank and I had been going through a rough patch. He worked all hours of the day and night, trying desperately to make a name for himself. We lived in a lovely two-story house with a pool. I'm not proud of it but I'm afraid the guy who serviced the pool also started to service me. Dana was his name. God he was gorgeous. Anyhow one thing led to another. Frank came home early one night and caught me and Dana *in flagrante delicto*, as they say. We'd been upstairs in the guest bedroom doing lines. I expected Frank to be furious, but the truth is he stripped down and joined us, coke and all. Turned out old Frank was a wanna be bisexual under the covers. He'd just never come out of the closet."

Ralph topped off all three glasses of wine. He glanced at Heather. She seemed fascinated by Kat's lurid narrative.

"Go on," urged Ralph. "It must've been something of an epiphany."

"I'll say it was," said Kat, taking a big gulp of her wine. "But kinda beautiful at the same time. You know what I mean? It was like a feast of the senses, and I was the main dish. Except when they were doing each other I mean but then I was treated to a visual demonstration you wouldn't believe. I don't want to offend your sensibilities but two men rutting and grunting while the wife looks on is incredibly stimulating."

Ralph looked over at Heather. Heather was loving it. He thought he heard Heather let out a little moan.

"Frank got up and left the room," continued Kat. "Dana wasn't finished, God, he was insatiable. I was helping him with my mouth when we heard a crash. Frank had fallen down the stairs and lay in a heap at the bottom, buck-ass naked. We got dressed and dialed 911 but Frank was dead by the time the ambulance arrived. The cops got there about the same time. They questioned Dana and me but there wasn't much we could add. Three weeks later they arrested me and Dana."

Kat took another gulp of her wine. She had a drawn expression on her face. Ralph replenished Kat's wine. Then he poured the rest of the bottle into his glass. Heather was doing fine.

"Long story short, I was sent to the women's detention center in Raleigh to await trial," said Kat softly. "Dana and I were each other's alibis, but the cops weren't buying it. I should've mentioned the fact earlier that Dana's black. That didn't work in his favor. My charges were eventually dismissed because there was insufficient evidence to convict, but Dana was charged and convicted of first-degree murder. He swore he was innocent. Didn't matter. They sent him to the Nash County Correction Center where he's currently serving a life sentence. And that's who I really am. I don't suppose you'll want me as a roommate after this. I should be going. Thank you for a lovely evening."

"Sit down, sweetheart," said Heather, pulling Kat back down on the sofa. "In the first place you shouldn't be driving after all that wine. In the second place I can't imagine going through all that and still being able to hold your head up high. And in the third place I'm fascinated by something you said. About Frank being a closet bisexual and all. Ralph's probably gonna lose his shit and maybe I've had a teensy bit too much wine myself, but you've been honest with us, and I want to be honest with you. I've always wondered what it'd be like to make love to a woman."

Ralph was flabbergasted. Kat not so much.

"Funny you should ask," smiled Kat. "While I was in the women's detention center, we didn't have much choice when it came to sexual partners. I don't want to brag but I got to be pretty good at eating pussy."

"Would you mind showing me?" asked Heather shyly. "I'm sure Ralph wouldn't mind."

"Better than that," said Kat, squeezing Ralph's hand. "Ralph can join us. I think we've all had enough wine to sufficiently lubricate the process."

It turned out Kat had a surprisingly talented tongue for a grocery clerk. Heather was an eager initiate. And Ralph was a happy guy.

The next morning, they tumbled out of the king size bed and went their separate ways. Before they parted, they all agreed that an ongoing relationship was a definite possibility. The rent wasn't due for another three weeks on Ralph and Heather's apartment and Kat said she had to give notice at her current address. Meanwhile another get-acquainted dinner date was set for the following Monday evening. In case they'd left anything out.

That evening at dinner Heather was awfully quiet.

"What's the matter, sweetheart?" asked Ralph. "I thought last night went particularly well."

"I just wish you hadn't told her about our retirement account," said Heather. "I mean I trust Kat and all, but I don't think it's a good idea to brag about it. You know what I mean?"

"I wasn't bragging about it," said Ralph defensively. "After all she told us some amazing details about her private life. I wanted to tell her something in return. It isn't exactly a secret. When mother died, she left me her entire estate which amounted to $50,000 and change. I cashed it all in and bought bit coins. You didn't think that was wise. In fact, if you recall that was our first real fight. Then bit coins went up, I cashed out at the peak, and we ended up with $450,000 which I invested in a mutual fund for our retirement. End of story. Maybe it was the wine doing the talking. I had more than my share."

"Well, maybe it's okay," admitted Heather. "After all it's where nobody but us can get to it. Isn't that so?"

"Sure is, sweetheart. Trust me. So, stop worrying."

The following Thursday evening at 5:45 Kat Morgan was sitting patiently in her 2003 Honda Civic outside her room at the Raleigh Inn waiting for Dana's phone call. Kat didn't really have a day job at the Food Lion, although what she'd told Ralph and Heather wasn't precisely a lie. She had worked at a local Food Lion not that long ago. She was discreetly dismissed when several mysterious discrepancies showed up on her cash register transaction history. Nobody could prove there was a problem, but it appeared Kat's cash register had recorded ten times as many individual item refunds as any other register in the store during the previous week.

HR did a belated background check and came across her arrest record in Orange County. Not for the murder, that was old news. Besides she'd never been convicted, and that record had been automatically expunged. No, the offense for which she was charged had to do with a non-violent misdemeanor at the Durham Walmart where she was arrested for shop lifting. Kat claimed she was taking a belated employee-discount on several articles of clothing by virtue of her status as an unpaid employee at the self-checkout register. The charges were eventually dismissed but they were never expunged.

Kat's room at the Raleigh Inn was both her abode and her workplace. Kat played for pay during most afternoons and on occasion into the wee small hours of the morning. She didn't want Dana to call her in the room because she was sure the phone was bugged. Kat was nobody's fool. Her cellphone rang. After proceeding through the rigamarole that precedes inmate connection with the outside world, Dana answered at his end.

"Hey Babe, how you doing?"

"Good, baby, how about you?"

"Can't complain given the circumstances. You put anything on my book this week? I'm running short on toothpaste."

Dana's "book" was his Inmate Trust Fund Account. Kat replenished Dana's book on a weekly basis. It never seemed to be enough for his "toothpaste" needs!

"I did this morning, baby. Check out the balance. Got some good news. You're gonna love it!"

"What happen, Babe? You win the Lotto?"

"Better than that, baby. I think we hit the motherfucking jackpot!"

"Give me details, Babe, but do the short version. We only got fifteen minutes."

Kat related her Monday evening visit with Ralph and Heather, omitting the salacious details of their postprandial romp.

"You recall Mike Peterson?" asked Kat. "You asked me to do the research. Mike did time at Nash. He was supposed to be a lifer, but they released him on time served after eight years. Mike's lawyers advised him to submit an Alford Plea. HBO did a series about it. Problem with us is we ran out of cash before we ran out of options. Frank only left a hundred thou insurance and that got eaten up before your case went to trial. You been telling everyone you're innocent, right? That's the deal with an Alford plea. You continue to insist you're innocent, but you're willing to plead guilty to a lesser charge. Here's the bulletin. My boy Ralph got $450 big ones tucked away in a mutual fund. That number pays a lot of legal fees to get the wheels of justice turning. I think I can crack Ralph's safe. Trust me on this one, baby."

"Good news, Babe. We coming up on eight years' time served next June. Shit, I can hold my breath that long. Pursue the plan, Babe. Don't tell me till it's done. Love you, Babe. Chat next week."

Friday morning at 10:35 Ralph received a text from Kat.

Good morning Ralph even though I hardly know you there's something about Heather I need to share. I'm a busybody by nature and it has more than once gotten me into trouble. Sometimes I poke my nose in where it doesn't belong but I detest people who lie to me. After I got home from our late Monday night/early Tuesday morning tryst I used an app I found on the dark web to explore Heather's background. She's not who she pretends to be Ralph. I won't say more until I have confronted her directly. After all I may be totally wrong but I don't want to see you hurt. I've grown fond of you since our encounter. Intimacy does that to me. As an aside you have a magnificent cock, sir, and I look forward to once again partaking of its delightful nectar come Monday. You will come again Monday for me I trust? Be gentle with me my handsome stranger. I fear I may be falling in love.

Ralph was on his coffee break in his office at Dick's Sporting Goods at the time. At first, he shrugged the text off. He barely knew Kat whereas Heather was an open book. To be sure, there was that wild time before they met. Well, that's actually how they met but Heather had made some big changes in her life since then. Ralph was pretty sure about that. He did think Kat was sincere in her remarks about the magnificence of Ralph's package. No woman he'd known intimately had ever remarked on it before, but you know what they say about taste. And speaking of taste Kat tasted pretty good her own self. Ralph wasn't the least bit concerned about Kat's purported suspicions, but he decided to keep the text. It couldn't hurt. Could it?

Saturday morning at 11:17 Ralph received another text from Kat. This one contained links and pictures. Heather was out shopping. Ralph went into his office and closed the door.

Hey handsome it's Kat again. I just wanted to bring you up to speed on my text from yesterday morning. I texted Heather and told her what I'd discovered about her perfidious behavior. I fully expected her to deny the whole thing. She told me in so many words to mind my own goddamned business. She said she had a good thing going and I wasn't gonna fuck it up. She said she enjoyed having her pussy eaten by a pro, but if I ever tried to come between her and her man, she would fuck me up big time. I can show you a screenshot of the text exchange between us if you like. I'm sorry to break the news, sweetheart, but I think Heather is only after your money. I've forwarded the results of my research to you. Make your own decisions based on the hard facts, my darling, but I think your Heather is trouble.

Following the text were links to a variety of seedy websites. Uncle Randys Erotic Review. The American Sex Circus. Fantasy Kink Relief. Remarkable Rubs. Ralph remembered Remarkable Rubs. That was the old website where he had first met Heather. He thought they'd gone out of business. He clicked on the link. Sure enough, there was a younger Heather in all her glory. She was wearing a smile and very little else. Ralph particularly remembered those nipples. He had to admit Heather Marsh had a pair of very serviceable nipples. He also had to admit Heather had put on a little weight since the good old days. She was still lovely though.

Ralph clicked on Uncle Randys Erotic Review. Yikes! Some dude named The Captain had written up a review dated three days ago describing in detail the sensual delights provided by a sensual massage therapist The Captain called Honeypot Sugarpie. The picture at the end of the review was naked from the neck down. You couldn't see her face, but the body sure looked like his Heather. Or her twin sister.

Randy clicked on The American Sex Circus. Up popped a collection of glowing testimonials regarding Honeypot Sugarpie and her remarkable skills when it came to squeezing every last drop out of, well you know. One of the blurbs contained an embedded link to a video. Ralph clicked on the link. He gasped. A naked lady on the bed in the video was adrift in the throes of ecstasy, her trembling legs spread wide. She was being vigorously humped by a man seen only from behind, but it was undeniably Heather Marsh's face, wreathed in smiles and panting for all she was worth.

Ralph was about to click on Fantasy Kink Relief when the door to his office opened and Heather waltzed in.

"Hi sweetheart am I interrupting anything?"

When she saw the porn video filling the screen she giggled.

"What are you watching? And why was your door shut? Honestly, you're beginning to act like a teenager. Here, let me see what you're slobbering over. The lady on the bottom looks vaguely familiar. Oh My God that's me!"

"I think you need to sit down for this," said Ralph. "Kat sent me a bunch of unsettling texts yesterday and this morning. She promised to send me screenshots of a compromising text thread between the two of you that proves your devious nature. I have no doubt such a thread exists. I don't want you to think I believe everything she told me, but I do think we need to clear the air."

"I don't much like Kat anymore," said Heather, sitting on the guest chair. "Regardless of the outcome of our little Come To Jesus moment, I vote to get rid of Kat. As far as our future is concerned that's a whole different can of worms. I'm ready for the inquisition."

"I'm only interested in the truth," said Ralph. "For example, the video we were watching. There's no doubt the lady on the bottom was you. Do we agree?"

Heather nodded.

"It sure looked like me," she said softly.

"Well, the guy on top was me," said Ralph. "You got in at the tail end of the show. Kat must've recorded our activities when she excused herself to go to the bathroom. I recognized the sheets on our bed when the video started. And the picture on our wall when the camera jiggled at one point. So that's one item out of the way."

"What a horrid thing to do," said Heather. "She must've planned this whole thing."

"There's more," said Ralph. "Kat is a very resourceful young lady. Well, maybe not so young. But she does know her way around the Internet. She sent me a screenshot of one of your old posts, from back when you were doing the rub stuff. The Remarkable Rubs website disappeared years ago but once something appears on the web vestiges of that something may remain for years in unrelated repositories. The web's memory is eternal."

"It was just a game to Kat," said Heather bitterly. "Winner takes all. Damn her to Hell anyway."

"There's more," said Ralph. "The posts on Uncle Randys Erotic Review and The American Sex Circus? Kat registered as The Captain. She posted those bogus reviews herself, including the link to the video."

"The bitch was determined to win," said Heather. "She sure went to a lot of trouble to sabotage our relationship. The stakes must've been pretty high."

"$450K to be exact, if my guess is right," said Ralph. "Wait, there's more. I saw a picture naked from the neck down on Uncle Randys Erotic Review that looked like you. Kat must've snapped a picture of you naked, probably at the same time she shot the video, and used Google Images to search the web for similar pictures that resembled your body type. Clever, no?"

"What about the text thread she threatened to share with you?" asked Heather. "You can't fake a text thread."

"You can if you have Google Voice," said Ralph. "Let's say you have a Google Voice phone number in one name, like Kat, and another in a different name, like Heather. You can put together a thread that looks like a legitimate conversation. Remember, the labels in a text thread come from entries in your contacts list."

"So where does that leave us?" asked Heather sadly. "I think you've explained Kat's behavior to our mutual satisfaction. I think we both agree that Kat's history. But what about us? Are we history as well? Did Kat succeed in destroying the trust in our relationship?"

Ralph reached over and took Heather's hand. He squeezed it gently.

"Bear with me," he said. "This may take some time. There's a big difference between Trust and Truth. Truth is binary. Truth demands proof. There are no shades of truth. Something is either true or false. If it's even the tiniest bit false it isn't true. The truth, the whole truth, and nothing but the truth. It's a tall order."

Ralph took a deep breath.

"Trust, on the other hand, is all encompassing," he continued. "I trust you regardless. You don't have to prove to me that you're worthy of my trust. Trust is earned over a long period of time. And trust is subjective. I trust you to tell me the truth, and you don't need to prove it."

"I think I understand so far," said Heather, holding on to Ralph's hand for dear life.

"Back in the bad old days when you were selling sexual services there was no truth involved. The plain truth is it was all fantasy. You told the client what he wanted to hear. When you said you wanted your client to come for you it wasn't necessarily true. Truth was you wanted to get it over with because you had another client waiting in the wings. Trust, however, was a whole different thing. Your client trusted you to arouse him to completion. You trusted him to pay you for that service. Up front, in most cases, or at the end if you'd known him for a long time."

Heather nodded slowly.

"Here's another example. The truth is we'll have many disagreements over the course of our relationship. I trust those disagreements won't destroy the relationship. I trust we will always find a way to come back together. The truth is I don't know for certain that will be the case. I simply trust that it will."

Heather closed her eyes. A tear trickled down her cheek.

"Here's another example. The truth is I want to marry you. I trust you want to marry me too."

Heather nodded. Then she opened her eyes.

"God, I love you Ralph," she sighed. "Of course, I want to marry you. But there's something I need to do first."

Heather whipped out her cellphone, scrolled through her contact list and selected Kat. She sent her a two-word text.

Checkmate, Bitch.

Hope Calls It a Day

It was autumn, the season for tying up loose ends and putting up preserves for the winter, or as they call it on Pleasure Island, the tail end of hurricane season. Pleasure Island is made up of three Atlantic Ocean beach towns: Carolina Beach, Kure Beach, and Fort Fisher. Pleasure Island sits at the far eastern tip of Interstate 40 which begins its eastward journey 2559 miles way out west in Barstow, California. I40 officially ends on the western outskirts of Wilmington, North Carolina, but if you keep going on the same road it doesn't peter out until you reach Snow's Cut Bridge.

Hope Kennedy was in the process of winding things down. She had standing orders with her scheduling service, Tess, not to accept new clients. These days Hope's occupational itinerary was down to six regulars for an hour each, every other week. She'd given up the lease for her office space on Independence Blvd. Now she worked primarily out of Gerald's third bedroom in the house on Kure Beach.

Still enthusiastically indulging in Hope's distinctive menu of quasi-therapeutic services were Millie and Harry who came on alternate Wednesdays. Benson was her Thursday rub. Hope did an outcall every other Thursday to see Benson, who was in hospice care ever since he'd had the stroke (which was not rub-related!). She had one other regular she enjoyed seeing, a guy named Sergei Kaufman, who also took care of Hope's Harley. Tess herself was the fifth. Tess never got tired of Hope's feminine touch. And then there was Gerald. Gerald was not limited to every other week. Gerald got as much Hope as he could handle.

Hope was having her second cup of coffee and browsing through the op-ed section of the Wilmington Star News when she heard a knock at the door. Strange. She had no clients scheduled for the day and Gerald had gone to work thirty minutes ago. She got up to answer the knock.

A brown-haired girl stood on the front porch. She had on a bright yellow T-shirt and denim shorts that hugged her skinny thighs. A dented Honda Civic was parked on the street in front of Gerald's house. The young girl looked frightened. She couldn't have been much older than eighteen.

"Can I help you?" asked Hope. The girl looked strangely familiar.

"Mom?" asked the girl nervously. "Are you Hope Kennedy? It's Faith."

"Faith?" said Hope, gathering the waif in her arms. "My Faith? Come in sweetheart. I'm so happy to see you. How long can you stay? Do your grandparents know you're here?"

"Nobody knows I'm here," sobbed Faith. "I woke up a week ago and I had this urgent need to get in touch with my real mom."

"How on earth did you find me?" asked a bewildered Hope. "I thought I was pretty well isolated from the rest of the civilized world."

"I left Myrtle Beach yesterday morning," said Faith, drying her eyes on her T-shirt. "Daddy told me about your website. www.HopeAbides.com. I looked it up. Your website needs work, by the way. The sliders are outdated, and the font is pathetic."

"What do you know about websites?" asked Hope, pulling Faith in and closing the door behind them. "Come into the living room where we can talk. Shouldn't you be in school? I'm so glad to see you."

"I graduated high school in June," said Faith, sitting down on the cluttered sofa. "I decided to take a year off school and learn about the real world. That was one of the reasons I had to find you. It was like this huge piece of my life was just missing."

Hope picked the magazines up off the sofa and sat next to Faith.

"The first thing you do, young lady, is call your grandparents and let them know you're okay," said Hope firmly. "They must be frantic with worry. I've never been close to that family, but I do know what it's like to lose a loved one."

"Okay, Mom," said Faith dejectedly. "But to be honest I don't think they really care where I am. They're always too busy with clubs and social shit to give a fuck about what I'm doing."

"And watch that mouth," said Hope with a grin. "You sound like me at your age. Do you want something to drink? I'll bring you a glass of fresh squeezed orange juice."

Hope went into the kitchen while Faith pulled out her cell phone and dialed home. When Hope returned Faith had just disconnected.

"You were right, Mom," Faith said. "Grams said they looked high and low for me all day yesterday. They were about to call the cops when I phoned. She says to tell you hi and wish it was under better circumstances. What did she mean by that?"

"Your adoptive parents and I have had our differences in the past," said Hope. "Not that they weren't warranted but that's all water under the bridge. The important thing is you're here now. How did you find me, by the way. My address isn't listed on the website and even if it had been it wouldn't have been this address. It would've been the address of my space on Independence Blvd. Or maybe even the apartment I used to share with Aretha Mae. You never did know about Aretha Mae, did you? She's the one who built my website in the first place. God, I've missed you."

"I called the phone number on the 'Contact Me' pull-down tab on your website," said Faith. "When some lady named Tess answered I told her my name and said I was trying to find you. She said you weren't taking on new clients anymore. I said I was your daughter. By the way, Mom, I browsed through your website. Some of the services you advertise aren't listed on any Therapeutic Massage website I've ever visited. Wanna dish?"

"We can catch up later," grinned Hope. "Not sure if you're ready for a full-blown history lesson from your mom's past. It ain't all pretty."

"Anyhow this Tess asked me a few leading questions to make sure I wasn't a fake," continued Faith. "I guess I passed the test because she gave me your Kure Beach address. That was yesterday afternoon. After we disconnected, I had second thoughts about coming to see you. Like what if you didn't remember me or, even worse, what if you didn't want to see me at all? I called Tess back and told her about my fears. She said it might be a good idea if I met one of your friends first. She gave me the phone number of Aretha Mae Jackson who lives on Figure Eight Island. Aretha Mae invited me out to her place for dinner. She stays with some guy named Jerry something. Jerry is a hoot. He kept offering me twenty-dollar bills. Do you know what that's all about?"

"Aretha Mae's friend, Jerry, is a kidder," said Hope. "But he's okay. So, what did you do next? Oh, wait a second I forgot to ask. What's your dad doing these days?"

"He's a fitness trainer at one of those health clubs in North Myrtle Beach," replied Faith. "He dates lots of girls, but I don't think he'll ever settle down."

"I understand," said Hope. "Once you've experienced the best in the west you can never settle for second best. So anyhow, you had dinner with Aretha Mae and Jerry. Do they have a nice place?"

"It's fucking huge, Mom," gushed Faith. "And Jerry treats Aretha Mae like she's some sort of princess. I didn't think she looked all that hot, to be honest."

"You've never seen her in a G-string, sweetheart," said Hope wryly. "Continue."

"We had dinner and sat around and talked until maybe midnight," said Faith. "Aretha Mae made up the bed in the spare room. When I woke up this morning she was gone. Off to tend the last of her sea turtles, I guess. Anyhow Jerry gave me your address and here I am."

"How long can you stay, sweetheart?" said Hope. "We've got a lot of catching up to do."

"As long as you want me to, Mom," said Faith, reaching over and giving her mother a big hug. "It's been such a long time."

When Gerald got home that evening, he was surprised to discover that they had a new guest; a live-in, long-lost daughter named Faith, who he welcomed with open arms.

They did not live happily ever after. Nobody lives happily ever after. But staying alive with someone you love is way ahead of what's in second place. LYFFR. (Love You Freakily Forever Regardless). Have a kick ass day!

Acknowledgments

I wish to first thank my wife, Mary Ann. After forty years and counting she's still the one.

This is my seventeenth literary work. Which is a little messed up because I originally set out to write six. Somewhere along the line I got distracted by the allure of life. Imagine that in a boy born in Montana, an aging Virgo, and an ex-computer programmer all rolled up in one sturdy, peasant body. Emphasis on the sturdy.

A massage practitioner named Hope suggested to me during a pummeling session that I may be interested in telling her story. I've never turned down a challenge. And dang if it wasn't a wonderful idea.

The inimitable Joyce Gornie knocked one out of the park with her careful attention to detail as she read and reread each draft and spent hours redlining my mistakes. A new lady named Holly jumped into the fray and proved her worth immediately. Thanks, Holly. Nikki Bountiful is the best muse a guy could ever ask for. God bless them all!

And finally, I can't thank the inventors of the Internet enough (Al Gore included!) for making research accessible to everyone, even those of us who don't have close, interpersonal relations with obscure archaeologists. I apologize to anyone if I inadvertently purloined or plagiarized your material because I couldn't find the material's origin. If you let me know it's yours, I'll ask permission to use it and if you won't give me your permission, I'll remove the offending element(s). If you grant me your permission to use it, I'll include attribution and eternal gratitude in the Acknowledgements section of the next edition of this book. Promise.

I won't promise there won't be an eighteenth book. I've lost all control over my creative output. But I will say this. I do enjoy writing and I know this much is true. It's always darkest just before they pull the plug.

Cheers!